How Lovely To Be a Woman

Stories and Poems

Tiffany Michelle Brown

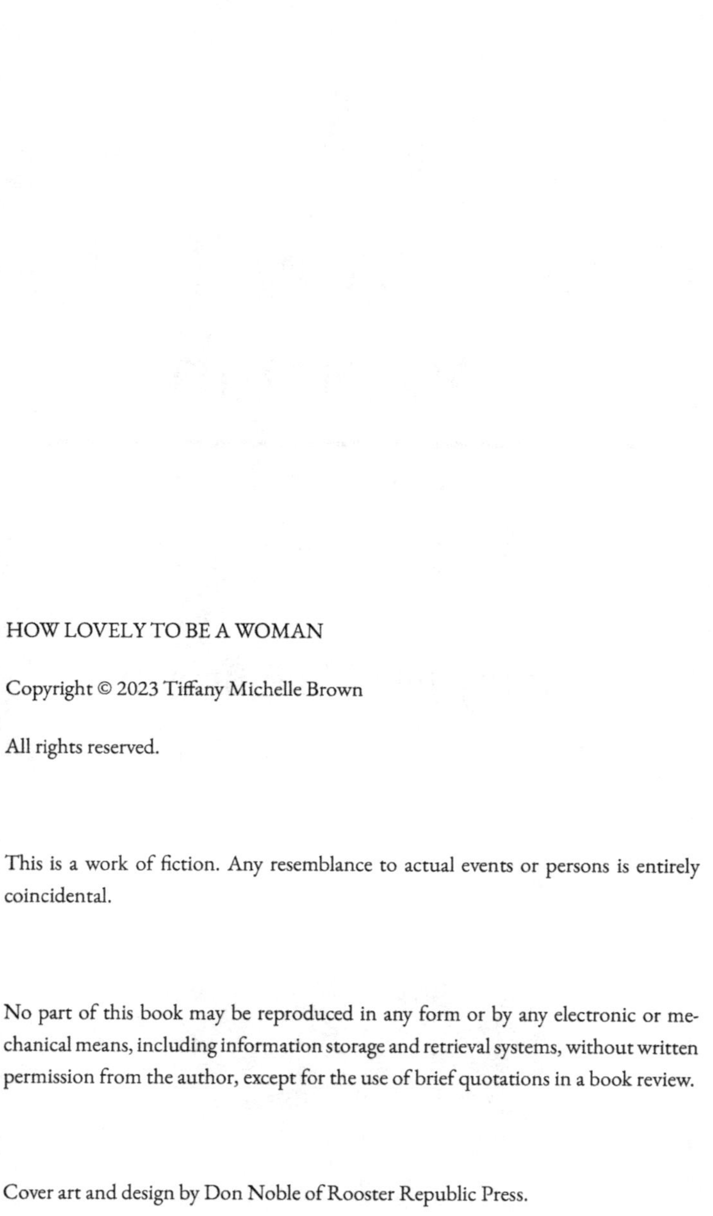

HOW LOVELY TO BE A WOMAN

Cover art and design by Don Noble of Rooster Republic Press.

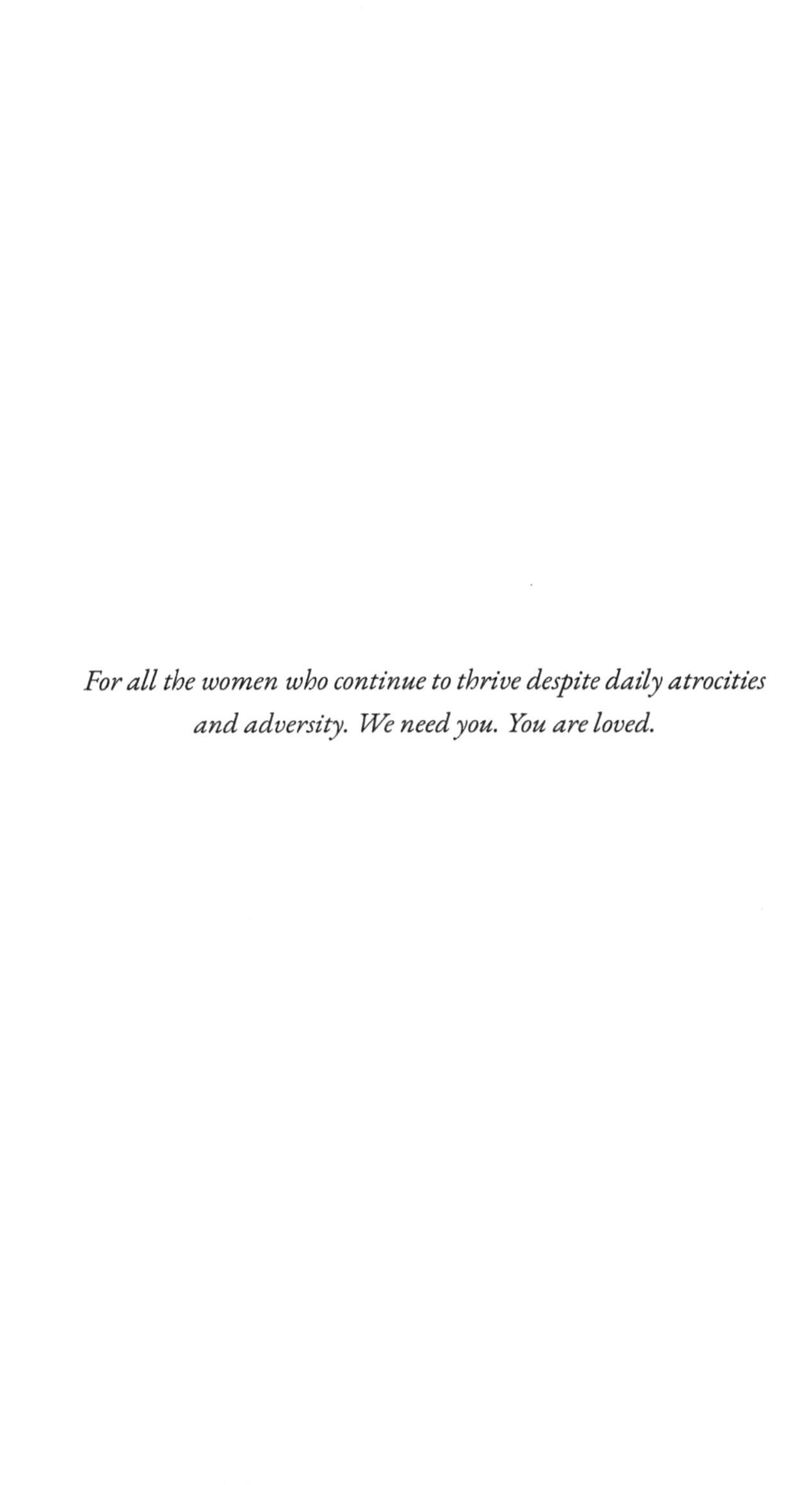

For all the women who continue to thrive despite daily atrocities and adversity. We need you. You are loved.

Author's Note

A full list of content warnings are available in the back of this book.

This collection is written by a white, cisgender, het(ish) woman of privilege, so it's worth noting that the experiences of womanhood explored within this book are nowhere near all-encompassing.

Readers, I implore you to seek out additional works that explore gender by BIPOC and LGBTQIA+ authors and creators, including nonbinary and genderfluid folks, to fully understand the spectrum of oppression, resilience, and joy they experience while simply navigating the world as themselves.

We need to do better for every intersection of womanhood and personhood. We can't settle for anything less.

Contents

Foreword

The first time I met Tiffany Michelle Brown was in print. I read her story, "My Love, In Pieces," in an anthology we were both in called *Quoth the Raven: A Contemporary Reimagining of the Works of Edgar Allen Poe*. I was immediately struck by the seamless combination of viscera with love, the heartbreak of the narrator paired with the ghastliness of his actions. It was a standout story in an entire anthology of strong work.

Tiffany and I have spoken quite a bit thanks to that anthology. We were both in a Facebook group for the anthology's authors, but began speaking to each other outside of that space—on our own Facebook timelines, on other social media channels, through email, and starting during the pandemic, on Zoom. As of this writing, Tiffany and I have never met in person, yet our friendship is as close as any I've had offline.

Our friendship has included reading each other's work, something I do with pleasure and would do even if she and I had never talked outside of the Quoth the Raven Facebook group. Tiffany's work is almost a genre all its own, an artful blend of the macabre and the sweet, the quiet and the angry, all written with a deftness of hand I admire and am surprised by with each new story.

That talent is on full display in the collection you hold in your hands, a debut collection that I've been anticipating ever since Tiffany told me about it during one of our monthly chats. *How Lovely to Be a Woman* is a tour de force of feminist horror, a myriad of terrors that rip through your psyche like strips of wax from your skin. There are workplace grievances and desperate mommies-to-be, recreational killers and summoners of birds. As fantastic as the stories and their characters may seem, every single story contains something we can relate to—as women, as marginalized others, as people who don't have to make something up to create something to be afraid of. We already live this fear every day.

Tiffany's work always impresses, and *How Lovely to Be a Woman* is no different. It's every bit as lovely as its author.

Sonora Taylor
February 21, 2023

The Price of Motherhood

For the bargain price of $79,999.95, which she would pay in monthly installments of $99.95 for the next 66 years (not including interest), Leslie Dawson became a mother.

The day the courier arrived, Leslie wore her most responsible-looking outfit, which she'd bought at Goodwill especially for the occasion: a blue button-up, khaki pants, and a string of fake pearls. The cotton material was stiff and scratchy, but Leslie resisted the urge to change into her regular uniform of jeans and a T-shirt. She knew first impressions were important. She needed to resemble the epitome of domesticity today, even if only for a paid delivery person.

When she heard footsteps ascending the stairwell in her apartment complex, Leslie leaped from the couch and opened her door before the representative from Lyfelike had the opportunity to knock.

On the threshold, Leslie's smile dropped, and her heart clenched. She hadn't expected her baby to arrive in a silver, egg-shaped case that reflected the cheap fluorescents in the hall-way. When she'd pictured this day in her mind, she'd imagined the courier showing up with the baby strapped to their chest via a Baby Bjorn or pushed in a stroller. There had *never* been an egg.

"Leslie Dawson, it's a pleasure. My name is Matthew, and I'm from Lyfelike. Are you ready to meet your daughter?" The man shoved the egg toward her, zooming right past pleasantries and straight to business. The abruptness left Leslie rattled, and she simply stared until the silence grew awkward.

She cleared her throat and gave him a warm smile. "Absolute-ly. Won't you come in?" She'd made Crystal Light lemonade and microwaved some cookies she'd found on sale at the grocery store.

"I'm afraid I can't," Matthew said, his voice warm and boom-ing. "It's against company protocol. But I do have a few instruc-tions to share and of course, I'll stay long enough to ensure all is in order."

Leslie hazarded a glance down the hallway. Matthew was quite loud, and she was afraid one of her neighbors would emerge to *shoosh* them. And what would they see? Why, they'd see this man handing her a huge silver egg while she stood there dumbly in her imposter pearls. Leslie's cheeks flushed as she took the egg from Matthew.

"Is it okay for me to set this down?" she asked. "It's a bit heavy." It wasn't, but she longed to tuck the egg inside the apartment. Safe from prying eyes.

"Of course. While you do, a few instructions. Inside the package, there's a manual. It's *very* important that you read the manual, front to back, and dial in all of your preferred settings via your smartphone before you initiate your daughter's heartbeat."

Leslie blinked. Initiate her heartbeat? What the hell did that mean?

Her face must have betrayed her confusion, because Matthew gave her a good-natured chuckle. "It's not a difficult process, I assure you. It'll make sense once you've read the manual. Again, make sure you dial *everything* in beforehand as certain settings can only be adjusted by our team after she's alive. We can, of course, help you troubleshoot any issues you encounter, but in extreme cases, we'd have to reset her completely, and that would mean a reversion back to factory settings." Matthew filled his lungs with fresh air. "It's a pain."

Clinical. Technical. Purchased.

The words beat around inside Leslie's skull like an unwelcome ping pong ball. This was *not* the experience she'd hoped for—or what had been promised on that late-night infomercial she'd seen last year. Lyfelike billed itself as a company that created artificial intelligence entities that were more human than robot. Less computer, more life.

So where was the warmth? Where was the sweep of emotion she'd expected to feel? Matthew's instructions were stripping her resolve. Did she really want this?

She decided she would call Lyfelike later to ask about their return policy. For now, she'd pay attention and be agreeable—don't shoot the messenger and all. While Matthew's bedside manner could use some work, Leslie figured he was following a script, and she couldn't fault him for doing his job.

"Okay, got it." Leslie nodded, hoping she looked attentive and capable.

"That all being said, there are a few settings that may shift naturally as part of your daughter's programming. This will be in response to stimulus, learning, development, that sort of thing. After all, your daughter is meant to be very Lyfelike." He accentuated the final word, and Leslie resisted the urge to roll her eyes. "We want you to enjoy the full spectrum of the parenting experience, so be sure you give her the same level of care you would a human baby. You can monitor all of her settings in the Lyfelike app, and if they shift, refer back to the manual to see what she needs. If you have questions, call our customer service team."

"Sounds good."

"Would you like to ensure your daughter's appearance meets your expectations?"

Dear God, did he just ask her that? And did he expect her to check off a list or something? Blue eyes, great! Freckle on her temple. Yep, just where I requested it.

This was all way too weird.

Matthew smiled pleasantly, and beneath his congeniality, Leslie detected determination. He wouldn't leave until she'd opened the egg and proclaimed all was as it should be. Shit.

Leslie squatted next to the door and cracked open the silver case. The baby was nestled in purple silk and swaddled in soft cotton. Dark curls swooped across her forehead, the perfect frame for her round, pudgy face. Even in the shabby light of the apartment, her skin looked soft as rose petals.

Leslie felt tears building behind her eyes. A smile overtook her lips.

This is what she'd been waiting for. *This* is what she'd had in mind when she'd placed the order with Lyfelike twelve months prior. All of her reservations melted away as she gazed at the infant.

She swatted at her eyes and peered up at Matthew. "She's perfect."

The startup manual was one hundred and seven pages long, the type was small, and the wording was overly technical. Leslie read ten pages before a sharp pain flashed through her forehead and she realized she was squinting. To make matters worse, she hadn't retained a single word. She'd have to start again.

Leslie made herself a cup of tea, grabbed a sleeve of mini donuts, and flipped back to the beginning of the manual. At page twenty, Leslie pushed back from the table and sighed. She circled her shoulders, trying to release tension from her body. She'd been more successful this time around, but her progress was slow. She doubted she'd be able to read the manual in a single sitting. At this rate, it would take days.

She looked at Annalea, her new daughter, resting on a kitchen chair nearby. She was still swaddled, still "sleeping"—in Leslie's mind, this sounded much better than "not yet powered up." Urgency skittered through her fingers.

She picked up her phone, and powered up Instagram. As if the universe knew exactly what she was looking for, Ryan's latest post appeared at the top of her timeline, a family portrait that made her throat close. Ryan had his arm around his new wife, Pauline, a redhead with freckles who somehow managed to look effortlessly beautiful all the time. She held their one-year-old boy, Cash, in her long arms. The boy looked nothing like his mother and everything like his father. Leslie could see Ryan in the slope of the boy's nose, the dark shock of hair that crowned his head, his ice-blue eyes.

As Leslie stared at the picture, something cracked deep within her.

She crammed the last donut in her mouth, licked powdered sugar from her fingers, and closed Instagram. She launched the Lyfelike app and searched through its interface. There had to be a quick-start guide somewhere, right?

Thirty minutes later, Leslie had scoured the website to no avail. In their FAQs section, there was a question about quick-starts, but all it said was to read the manual in full before initiating the heartbeat.

This is some bullshit, Leslie thought, her frustration building. How did anyone have the patience to go through all of this? She'd already waited longer for her daughter to arrive than if she'd actually been pregnant. She needed to be a mother *now*.

On the home screen, Leslie tapped the "Initiate Setup" button. A warning popped up. Had she read the manual in full? It was an imperative step in the process, and blah, blah, blah... Leslie closed the window. The app informed her that the configuration would take fifteen minutes to complete.

Fifteen minutes, Leslie thought. *In fifteen minutes, I'll meet my daughter.*

Some of the settings were easy to choose. Leslie only wanted to change diapers five times a day and she could schedule their frequency down to the minute. She also wanted her daughter to sleep a full eight hours each night. The choices for temperament, goals, and bonding style were more esoteric, but Leslie chose with her gut.

She could read up on all of these choices later. Besides, Lyfelike had a customer service team. If there were any major errors, she would ask them to be fixed. She was certainly paying the company enough—and with money she didn't truly have—so she expected fantastic service.

Temperament? Good-natured, because who doesn't love a good-natured baby?

Life goal? Peace, which was vague, but sounded more than okay.

Bonding style? Secure, of course.

Fourteen minutes later, Leslie's thumb hovered over "Initiate Heartbeat." A single tear slid down her cheek as she tapped the screen and waited.

Leslie's phone chirped, announcing a new notification. She balanced Annalea in the crook of her left arm and held her phone close to her face. She'd surpassed two hundred likes on her latest

Instagram post, and the sudden sweep of validation made her blood hum.

Leslie had nearly forgotten how incredible it felt to be recognized.

Following her Lyfelike purchase twelve months prior, Leslie had abstained from posting to social media with any kind of regularity. She'd still post from time to time, but only strategically angled headshots or photos of knick-knacks in her cramped apartment. Never a full body shot. Never anything telling. She wanted Annalea to be a complete and utter surprise.

She also didn't plan to tell anyone her daughter was from Lyfelike. Rather, she'd tell everyone she'd successfully conceived thanks to a sperm donor.

She'd done the work, and now it was time to shine.

She'd taken nearly forty photos, trying to snap the perfect selfie and then using her smartphone's timer to get a better angle and wider shot. Throughout the photoshoot, Annalea stretched in her swaddling. She smacked her lips as she slept. Her little chest rose and fell. It was easy to believe she was made of blood and bone rather than metal and wiring.

Seconds after the upload, Leslie's phone erupted with congratulations and compliments. And now, a comment from Ryan: "She's beautiful, Les. We couldn't be happier for you. Motherhood looks good on you."

For the past two years, whenever she thought of Ryan, Leslie had heard him in her head telling her that it was okay, they weren't meant to have children. He still loved her.

Then, that IVF was far too expensive; even if they were successful, would they be able to financially care for their child amid all the medical bills?

Finally, he didn't love her anymore. Her obsession with motherhood had dulled her, turned her into someone else, someone he didn't know. He'd found Pauline. He was going to marry her. They were expecting a son.

But now, Leslie could replace all of those whispers of the past with newfound validation: *Motherhood looks good on you.*

She poured herself a glass of boxed wine, snuggled into the couch with Annalea on her chest, and closed her eyes. It was the first moment of peace she'd experienced in two years.

Leslie scrolled through the Lyfelike app as Annalea wailed in her arms. For something so small, she certainly had volume—volume Leslie hoped she could decrease or even mute. That had to be possible with AI, right?

She couldn't find volume settings, but she did discover a list of sound selections. She flipped through them as the baby continued to cry, the pitch, timbre, and octave switching as she touched her screen. Every choice grated her nerves.

How had it come to this? How, when everything had started so well?

The first two months had been bliss. Leslie's neighbors assumed she'd adopted a baby and lavished her with gifts for the newborn—patterned onesies, jar after jar of baby food, a breast pump (a well-meaning gift, but completely superfluous), home-cooked meals, everything she could possibly need as a new mother. Of course, Leslie let them believe what they wanted to and happily accepted each gift.

She delighted in feeding Annalea pureed peas and sweet potatoes during their first month as mother and daughter, though nourishment was entirely optional for Lyfelike infants. She dressed Annalea in darling outfits festooned with roses and ruffles and bows. She even enjoyed tending to Annalea's diaper changes since she knew exactly when her daughter would need a fresh one *and* whether she'd be going number one or number two. Before bed each night, Leslie consulted the Lyfelike app to ensure her daughter was "well," which of course meant functioning properly.

However, as the surprise and novelty of Annalea's arrival wore off, Leslie found it difficult to stick to the routine she'd initially established. When the baby food gifted to her by her neighbors ran out, she didn't make an effort to purchase more. Since it wasn't a requirement, Leslie figured Annalea could do without.

She'd lost track of diaper-changing times, too. Yes, they happened every day with clockwork accuracy, but they were less of an *event* now. During the first few months, Leslie had anticipated Annalea's changing times, often placing the baby on her changing table and arming herself with a wipe before her daughter did her business. Now, she relied on the baby crying to tell her she needed a change.

And despite the sleep setting Leslie had selected before initiating Annalea's heartbeat, the baby had begun waking in the middle of the night. And when she woke, she cried and cried and cried.

Leslie finally consulted her Lyfelike app, which she'd also been neglecting as of late, and discovered that Annalea's settings had changed dramatically. Her Good-Natured temperament now read as Distressed. Her life goal was Survival. Her bonding style was Anxious-Preoccupied, whatever that meant.

And now, she wouldn't stop crying. Leslie changed Annalea's diaper, sang her a lullaby, spooned a bit of canned soup into her mouth, but nothing worked. Leslie didn't know what the hell the baby needed, and the constant bawling was driving her mad.

She scrolled to the bottom of the Lyfelike app, memorized the customer service number, and punched it into her phone. As the line rang, Annalea's blubbering grew more and more desperate, as if she somehow sensed in her little robot brain that her mother was about to complain about her.

Annalea's screams were so piercing, Leslie didn't hear the customer service rep when they came on the line. Or when they asked how they could help. She didn't hear a thing until the rep started spouting off a scripted goodbye: "Thank you for calling Lyfelike, where we bring home to you." And then the line went dead.

"Dammit," Leslie shouted and chucked her phone onto the couch. She marched to the bathroom, Annalea in her arms. She set the baby on the tile floor, her jaw clenched in frustration, her breath coming hard through her nose.

Annalea's face was red and splotchy. A pang of guilt shot through Leslie like lightning.

Damn the people at Lyfelike for doing this. For making Annalea so convincing. For making Leslie feel like a godawful mother.

Leslie caught her reflection in the dark glass above the sink. She looked like hell. There were bags under her eyes, her hair looked like a motel for rodents, and her lips were turned down in an exhausted grimace.

"I just need a minute," she said, her voice trembling.

She left the bathroom and closed the door behind her.

"It sounds like she'll need a manual override," the Lyfelike rep said over the phone. "I'm looking at her settings right now. Any idea how this happened?"

"None," Leslie said. "I've taken exceptional care of her." The lie was oily on her tongue, but she wasn't about to be lambasted by a customer service rep for her parenting skills.

"Okay, let's get someone out to you as soon as possible."

"That sounds wonderful," Leslie said.

"Looks like the earliest appointment we have available is Wednesday between 9 AM and 1 PM."

Leslie frowned. Why did it feel like she was scheduling an appointment to have a contractor over to fix a leaky faucet? And two more days of having to deal with a malfunctioning robot baby? Unacceptable.

"You don't have anything sooner?" Leslie tried hard to keep the edge out of her voice, but it was there, sharp and dark.

"You could contact our ServicePro team," the rep said. "They would likely be able to send someone out to you today."

Relief flooded through Leslie, but before she could say yes, this was exactly what she wanted, the Lyfelike rep continued. "However, access to our ServicePro team is only available for an additional fee."

Leslie's chest tightened. *You've got to be kidding me.* "And that fee is...?"

"$99.95 per call, ma'am."

"Are you serious?" Pain sliced through Leslie's temple, the onset of a stress migraine. "One hundred dollars for a single call? Even though I'm already paying you that much monthly?"

"It's a separate service, ma'am."

"How is this ethical? You're dealing with people's *lives* here! And stop calling me ma'am. It's condescending." Leslie's voice was ragged. Her chest burned, and her whole body shook. "I bought something that was *really* expensive and that I shouldn't have purchased in the first place. It's not working out, and it shouldn't be this goddamn hard!"

Silence floated through the line as Leslie reined in her breathing.

"I'm sorry, Leslie. Can I call you that?"

"Sure."

"I'll submit this with a note that if any cancellations come through, your request receives priority. Unless, of course, you'd like me to connect you with ServicePro?"

"Does it sound like I want the help from ServicePro?"

"Understood, Leslie. Is there anything else I can do for you?"

"No."

"Thank you for calling Lyfelike, where we bring home to you."

Miraculously, after Leslie hung up, her apartment was blissfully quiet. She assumed that Annalea, much like real, human infants, had tired herself out. She would let her sleep as long as she needed.

In the interim, she'd do some research. Leslie flipped through the pages of Annalea's instruction manual until she found the section with setting descriptions.

A Distressed temperament was easy enough to understand. Annalea wasn't getting the level of care she needed, so she was fussy and irritable. It was meant to be a signal for the owner to increase their level of care and attention.

The Survival life goal meant that Annalea was doing whatever was necessary to thrive. Her independence and personal initiative were higher than they should be.

The Anxious-Preoccupied bonding style was characterized by four heavy phrases: emotional hunger, fantasy bond, lack of nurturing, and turbulence.

The manual slipped from Leslie's fingers and tumbled to the dirty carpet as realization struck her. She'd failed, hadn't she? Annalea's settings had shifted because she'd been doing a shitty job, not because the AI technology was malfunctioning. Leslie had wanted this for so long, and now...she couldn't cut it.

The air suddenly felt suffocating in the apartment. Leslie ran to the nearest window, threw it open, and took five deep breaths.

Could she turn this around? Surely she could learn from this failure and strive to be better, right? She had to. She had to succeed at this.

She screwed her eyes shut and called forward her memories. The painful ones, the joyful ones, everything that had brought her to this moment. Making love to Ryan and feeling like this was it, the time they'd conceive naturally, only to see those two dreaded lines on a pregnancy test the following month. The bottles of wine she'd drowned in when he'd left her. That little stir of hope in her womb when she'd seen the Lyfelike infomercial. The way she'd finally felt complete when she first held Annalea in her arms.

She could do this. She could be a good mother. She simply had to remember and rebuild.

Leslie's phone dinged. She pulled the device from her pocket, opened Instagram, and squinted at the new photo posted on Ryan's account. The image was confusing at first. She was staring at a cropped body shot of a woman wearing jeans, her red T-shirt pulled up to expose her midriff. There was nothing exceptional or strange or disturbing or magical about the belly on display.

But when she read the caption, adrenaline threatened to scald her insides.

"Coming soon! We're hoping for a girl this time. #ProudPapa"

Pauline was pregnant again. The belly was hers, and beneath her creamy, freckled skin, a baby was growing inside her.

The newfound motivation Leslie had cultivated just moments ago dimmed. Her sense of failure flared anew.

Her body had betrayed her. Finances kept her from creating a family with the man she'd once loved. And now, Leslie had *bought* a child.

And for what?

She trudged to her kitchen, rifled through her cupboards, and pulled out the bottle of cheap gin she kept in case of emergencies. Leslie sunk into the couch cushions, staring at Pauline's belly and the joyous comments accumulating under the post. She tipped back the bottle until everything blurred.

Leslie awoke to the sound of someone screaming, a bright, shrill cry that jarred her senses. She tried to open her eyes, but the light streaming into her apartment was too harsh. Her pulse beat against her skull, and an unsettling pressure weighed heavily on her chest.

Was she having a panic attack? No, there was something on top of her. Something warm and moving.

Annalea!

Leslie forced her eyes open. Annalea's mouth was wide and angry as she bellowed, her breath hot on Leslie's face. A deluge of tears streamed down the baby's cheeks as she squirmed and kicked, trying to burrow deeper into the warmth of her mother.

But it was the state of her hands that sucked all the breath from Leslie's chest. Annalea's tiny palms were smeared with a red substance that resembled blood. A good deal of her fake skin had peeled back, revealing an intricate maze of metal and wiring. The mechanical digits flexed as they searched for Leslie's skin. When they found an acceptable entry point, the fingers dug in, and Leslie felt a flash of bright, hot pain shuttle through her.

Even as her discomfort intensified, Leslie gazed upon Annalea with wonder. Beneath the horror of the situation, another sensation welled up inside her, something strong and sure that she couldn't quite pinpoint.

"Sweet baby," she whispered. "My girl, my girl, my girl—"

Leslie pulled Annalea from her chest and sat up. Rivers of blood poured down her arms and slicked the skin beneath her T-shirt, but Leslie paid her injuries no mind. She was focused on Annalea. She bounced her baby and cooed, trying to get her daughter's cries under control. She wiped blood from Annalea's face, unsure if it was the synthetic stuff Lyfelike had injected into Annalea's stainless steel veins or her own. She examined Annalea's hands gently.

Her poor baby. Her poor, sweet baby.

And Annalea *was* hers, she reminded herself. This beautiful infant belonged to her, regardless of how she'd come by her. Screw all the pregnant bellies and people with more money and, therefore, access to biological science and everyone who knew how to do this parenthood thing right from the get-go. They had *nothing* to do with her relationship with Annalea. Absolutely nothing.

"It's okay, sweetheart," Leslie said, pulling Annalea closer still. "You found me. You found me, and I'm never letting you go."

Leslie swiped tears from her cheeks. She looked to the bathroom door, already knowing what she would find.

There was a hole in the door, the product of something scrabbling at the wood for hours on end. Smudges of red patterned the floor of Leslie's apartment, forming a trail from the bathroom door to the couch. Motherly pride capsized her heart.

She came for me, Leslie thought. *She needs me. She needs her mother. And I need her.*

As if in response, Annalea reached up and fisted the skin on Leslie's cheek. The infant's fingers disappeared beneath flesh. And in that moment, Leslie didn't feel pain. She felt something so much sweeter: connection.

It was a perfect moment, a moment that needed to be captured.

Wincing, Leslie lifted her phone and smiled.

Heavy Is the Head

You fear my crown,
The slithering mass of scales,
Probing tongues,
Snake eyes,
Obsidian orbs like so many dark stars,
Extinguished well before their time.

You hold your love at arm's length
Afraid of the marriage of fangs and flesh.
You're suddenly squeamish around blood,
Though we ran hot and fast,
Pulsing to the same beat,
Steadfast in the rhythm of our lives together
Before her betrayal
And my physical transformation.

I've always been monstrous, beloved,
But perhaps you were blinded by what
You considered

Beauty.

Do you not remember
How I slithered across your skin,
Swallowed you whole,
Wrapped myself around you tight enough to choke?

My reptilian brethren were always there,
Latched onto my heart,
Their venom singing through my veins.
Internal protection systems
Painted in muscle and viscera.
A part of me, always.

Now, I wear them,
Close enough to whisper truths in my ears
And turn liars and enemies to stone.

But you're safe,
Can't you see?

I've never turned you to marble
But you've hardened your heart.
You fear my crown,
But your dread is unfounded,
For you've never been able to see me at all.

Something Black

Lois decided that if Mr. Sharpe's eyes landed on her breasts one more time, she would simply walk out. "You see, sir, if we apply this simple calculation to our annual projections and then..."

Mr. Sharpe's eyes caught Lois's and then dropped to her chest. His gaze blazed through her taupe-colored cardigan. Instinctively, Lois shrank in her seat, wishing she could melt into the cushion. Existence as a wet spot—a stain—had to be better than this.

Finally, Mr. Sharpe turned and leaned in to examine the images on his computer screen. Lois could plainly see that he was surveying last month's earnings report, which her team had debriefed in full not an hour ago. He'd had no questions during the meeting.

Get up, Lois urged herself. *Get up and walk out.*

But Lois didn't, because she wasn't that kind of person. A frail woman more comfortable surrounded by numbers than people, Lois let her work do the talking for her. Her reports were careful, succinct, accurate, and quiet. In meetings, she strove to remain under the radar and waited until she was called upon.

She felt most comfortable in impersonal, gray-colored conference rooms, sitting in the corner. Lois fancied herself a workplace chameleon—someone who could blend in anywhere. Not because she wanted to adapt but because she wanted to get lost in her surroundings and disappear from view.

Lois had been with Sharpe Athletics for two years, satisfied to work away unnoticed in a corner cubicle in the Finance Department, as long as her paychecks continued to roll in. She knew her work was important, but she didn't need anyone to publicly acknowledge it.

The algorithm changed everything. It had been a happy mistake, something Lois stumbled upon while performing her regular duties. An associate in the Fabrication Department asked her to crunch some numbers in preparation for a customer sales promotion. Two hours later, Lois had not only produced the results her coworker had requested, she'd stumbled upon a predictive finance model—a special algorithm that, if applied correctly to their annual projections, could increase the company's profits while negating the company's bottom line by two percent.

"You need to show this to Jerry," David told her, leaning across the small partition into her cube. David had beautifully coifed hair, starched shirts, and a smile reserved for commercial actors. Lois was pretty sure she was in love with him.

"Really?" Lois asked.

"Call Heather. Get on his calendar." David winked at her. And damn that wink, Lois started to believe she should talk to the president of Sharpe Athletics.

The day of her discovery, Lois approached Heather's desk to set up a meeting with Mr. Sharpe, but when the pretty administrative assistant with pointed nails asked how she could help, Lois asked for directions to the bathroom. Heather's threaded brows knit together. She told Lois to walk down the hall, take a right, a left, and push.

In the bathroom mirror, Lois stared at her reflection. She gave herself a pep talk. "Go and ask for what you want. It's just a meeting."

When a toilet flushed nearby, Lois cut her pep talk short and slipped out of the bathroom before anyone could catch her talking to herself.

She took a deep breath and approached Heather's desk.

"Did you make it?" Heather drummed a pen on a notepad.

"Yes. Great directions." Lois smoothed a lock of brown hair behind her ear. "I'm...uh...I'd like to schedule a meeting."

Heather looked at Lois expectantly. "With Mr. Sharpe?"

Lois nodded.

"And what is this regarding?"

"The future of Sharpe Athletics," Lois said hurriedly.

Heather frowned. "Can you be a little more specific?"

"There's an..." Lois swallowed before continuing, "...algorithm I created that, uh, I think could really improve our profits. David said I should show it to Mr. Sharpe." Lois cringed inwardly for using her crush as a crutch.

"You're in Finance, right?"

Lois nodded.

"So, you'd like to propose a new financial strategy, is that correct?" Heather asked.

"Yes, yes, that's exactly it."

Heather's green eyes scanned her computer screen. She clicked her mouse a few times. "It looks like the next time he's free is two Wednesdays from now. Will half an hour be okay?"

"That should be fine."

"Okay, you're all set. The invite should be in your inbox."

"Thank you."

The worrying began as soon as Lois got back to her cubicle. What if she wasn't free during the time Heather had set up for her and Mr. Sharpe? Should she create a slide deck? How should she dress for the meeting?

"Did you get something scheduled?" David asked.

Lois jumped in her ergonomic chair and a stack of papers tumbled to the floor.

"I'm sorry. Didn't mean to startle you," David said, bending to pick up the papers. Lois admired flashes of well-developed bicep as he stretched to retrieve numbers and figures. A fine sheen broke out on her brow.

"I set up the meeting," Lois said, giving David a closed-lipped smile to hide her crooked teeth. She still held a grudge against her mother for not investing in braces for her when she was a child.

"Good for you, Lo."

Lois nearly tumbled into David's smile.

"Now, you prepare for the meeting and then you'll go in there and knock 'em dead. I know you will." David seemed so sure that everything would go well. It gave Lois confidence.

Per David's advice, she *did* prepare. Lois created a one-page recommendation outlining the company's current profitability model and what the profitability model *could* look like if they applied her algorithm. She selected her outfit carefully—a gray pencil skirt, a white button-up blouse, and a taupe-colored cardigan—an outfit she thought exuded professionalism.

She did not expect Mr. Sharpe to see anything sexual in it. She also didn't expect his inattention, which made it even more difficult than usual to form coherent sentences.

Lois cleared her throat and tried to conjure the words she'd so carefully rehearsed. "If we apply this simple algorithm, we will undoubtedly..."

Mr. Sharpe's phone rang and Lois started in her chair. Mr. Sharpe reached for the phone, picking up the receiver before the first long trill had concluded.

"Yes, Edward?"

Lois smoothed her skirt and looked around the office, not wanting to appear to eavesdrop.

"I see. I'll be right there."

Mr. Sharpe hung up the phone with a deafening click, put his hands on his knees, and pushed himself to standing. "Miss Connelly, I'm sorry to do this, but there's an issue in Fabrication that demands my immediate attention. I'm sure you understand."

Lois's mouth hung open, a lonely, soundless "o."

"See Heather and we'll pick this up again. Thanks for your time." Mr. Sharpe gestured toward the door.

Lois looked down at the black type of the recommendation she'd created. She hadn't even been able to supply Mr. Sharpe a copy. She fought the urge to rip the paper with her small hands, to cry. She rose, walked out of Mr. Sharpe's office, and waited in front of Heather's desk.

Mr. Sharpe bumped Lois's arm as he passed by her and strode down the hallway to a neighboring office, whistling all the way. Lois gripped the recommendation between her fingers, crinkling the paper.

She became suddenly aware of Heather's voice. "Hmm?"

"Do you need to reschedule?"

"Yes. When is he available again?" Lois asked.

"Two weeks."

"Two weeks," Lois repeated. She walked back to her desk and threw away her recommendation.

"How did the meeting with the boss-man go today?"

Lois turned and found David approaching her as she prepared to climb into her beat-up Civic. The wind threaded its fine fingers through his hair. He appeared particularly svelte jogging toward her. Lois wondered if he went to the gym.

"It was...it didn't," Lois mumbled.

David cocked his head to the side in confusion.

"Mr. Sharpe had to leave early," Lois explained. "I didn't really get to explain anything."

David shoved his hands in the pockets of his slacks. A sympathetic expression painted his face. "Sorry to hear that."

"I have another meeting," Lois said, fumbling with her keys, looking down at her hands. "In two weeks."

"That's how it goes, I guess. The higher-ups are always really busy."

Lois remembered Mr. Sharpe staring at her chest, then blatantly ignoring her. She opened her mouth to explain that this was something more when David lurched away from the car.

Lois frowned at him. "What's wrong?"

David pointed over Lois's shoulder. When she turned, she found a single crow perched upon the bike rack atop her car. Its black feathers brilliantly reflected the dwindling sunshine. The bird was staring directly at Lois. It opened its beak and let out four syncopated caws. Lois thought it sounded like it was choking.

"I don't think I've ever seen crows around here," David said, looking at the bird quizzically. "Must have something to do with the weather."

Lois fluttered her hand close to the bird and made shooing noises, but the crow remained fixed to its spot. "I'm sure it'll move when I start the car. I should go."

"Sure," David said. "See you tomorrow, Lo."

Lois climbed into the Civic and slammed the door harder than usual, hoping the noise would startle the bird. She didn't see anything fly away.

She turned the key in the ignition and peered up at the roof of the car, visualizing the crow that seemed so drawn to her, wondering if she should consider it a friend or foe.

For her second meeting with Mr. Sharpe, Lois wore a pair of navy blue slacks and a white button-up shirt. Cerulean drop earrings hung from her earlobes. She'd done some research on dressing for success. She'd read online that color blocking and wearing contrasting colors were two foolproof ways to appear in charge and confident. She had to admit, she felt more powerful than usual in the ensemble.

To prepare for round two, David offered to roleplay with Lois. Every couple days, they'd retreat to a conference room, and Lois would practice talking to "Mr. Sharpe." Of course, David could never accurately emulate their CEO. He was too attentive and understanding, urging her to talk more and more about her discovery. Lois always left their practice sessions feeling confident but also strangely deflated, because she knew her meeting with Mr. Sharpe, the *real* meeting, would never play out the way it did between her and David.

And she was right, because Mr. Sharpe was thirty-five minutes late. Lois sat awkwardly in the president's office, gazing out the window and tapping her pen against her notepad. A fresh copy of Lois's recommendation lay on Mr. Sharpe's desk.

This is it, Lois. He's ridiculously late. Walk out.

At that moment, Mr. Sharpe walked in. Without acknowledging Lois, he sat down in front of his computer and began scrolling through emails. Eyes glued to the screen, he said, "I'm sorry I'm late. I had another meeting that ran over. Had to put out some fires."

"I understand," Lois said. "Do you need a minute...or can I start?"

Mr. Sharpe sighed. "Actually, Miss...?"

"Connelly." He'd forgotten her name in two weeks' time?

"Miss Connelly, could we reschedule?" Mr. Sharpe gave her a taut smile. "I have another meeting in ten minutes, and I really need to prepare for it. I'm sure you understand."

A sharp *snap* sounded in the office. Lois looked down at her lap to find her pen broken in two, dark ink staining her hands and spilling like an oil slick across her lined notepad. "Oh, I..." She frantically gestured at her lap.

Mr. Sharpe hit a button on his phone and summoned Heather to his office. When she arrived, the administrative assistant quickly assessed the situation, plucked a tissue from the box on Mr. Sharpe's desk, and removed the dissembled pen from Lois's ink-mottled hands. She tossed it in the wastebasket, along with the tissue, and then said to Lois, "I'd hurry. That ink will stain. Not your skin so much, but your skirt."

Lois peered down at the black spot pooled on her lap, and her breath caught in her throat. As she rose and turned to leave, Mr. Sharpe called, "Be sure to reschedule with Heather."

The spot would not come out. Lois scrubbed and patted, but the ugly blob stayed put. The ink on her hands lightened considerably after a few washings with soap, but she still looked spotty, like a hesitant Dalmatian.

Lois was relieved David wasn't at his desk when she crept back from the bathroom. She knew he'd ask how the meeting went, and she'd have to admit that again, it hadn't gone well. Though she knew he'd reassure her, Lois was not in the mood to be placated.

She slumped in her chair and logged in. She opened an Excel spreadsheet and puttered about it for a few minutes.

A tapping noise drew her attention to the left, to the window near her desk that overlooked the cold concrete parking lot of Sharpe Athletics. On the window ledge, two crows tussled with each other, pecking the others' wings, emitting long, throaty caws, dangerously dancing along the slim ledge.

Is this some sort of strange mating ritual? Lois wondered. *Or is this a fight?*

One of the crows lunged forward, pecking its opponent close to its eye. The crow on the offensive squawked in pain, lost its footing, and plummeted backward away from the sill.

The victor ruffled its feathers and stretched its neck long and proud. The bird peered into the window directly at Lois, unblinking, strong, resolute. The sunlight reflected the dark matter of its wings, and Lois wished she could reach through the glass and stroke its feathers.

Lois marched down the hall with determination in her bones and rescheduled her meeting with Mr. Sharpe. She requested Heather schedule it at a time when Mr. Sharpe didn't have another meeting before or after the time allotted. She also made sure it wasn't close to lunchtime so the president couldn't dash off to a business meal. The meeting was set for a date one week away.

For the rest of the afternoon, Lois remained glued to her computer screen, working the way she did before she'd discovered the algorithm, with focus and resolve. When she logged off at quarter after five, she felt accomplished and had nearly forgotten about the horrible incident in Mr. Sharpe's office a few short hours ago. She decided she would shower the moment she got home to wash off the remnants of the ink and her bruised ego. Tomorrow would be a new day.

Though she'd managed to elude him the majority of the afternoon, David caught up with Lois in the parking lot.

As he approached her Civic, he looked about him and shook his head. "They're taking over the place," he said, gesturing to the throng of crows that sat atop the Sharpe Athletics headquarters. The horde sat in a neat line, wing to wing, appearing to watch the humans below from their elevated vantage point. Another grouping balanced on a telephone wire nearby. All were emitting agitated cries and shaking their feathers in the sun.

"It's a murder," David said.

"Excuse me?" Lois asked.

"A group of crows. It's called a murder."

"I wonder why," Lois said, peering up at the birds, admiring the deep black of their plumes. She thought they looked like sparkling onyx. And there was something graceful about the way they moved, craning their necks, shifting their weight. Something calculated and sure.

"Poetry, I think," David said, running a hand through his hair.

Lois wanted to reach out, pull his hand to her mouth, and lick it. She leaned against her car, trying to look cool, and cocked her head to the side instead. "Hmm?"

"I remember reading somewhere that people used to assign poetic names to animals and their groupings." David smiled at her. "I read something like that."

"It doesn't have to do with their violent tendencies?" The question slipped from Lois's lips before she was aware she was speaking. With the suggestion came a flash of the turbulent scuffle she'd witnessed that afternoon on the window sill.

David chuckled. "I don't remember any news stories about birds killing anyone."

"It was a stupid question," Lois said and fished for her car keys.

"How did today go? You getting a promotion sometime soon?"

The exuberance and hope in David's voice sucker-punched Lois in the gut. "He asked to reschedule, *again*, and I broke my pen. Spilled ink everywhere." She held up her hands, proof of her misfortune.

David reached out and took one of her hands to examine the spots. Lois's heartbeat blasted in her chest, and her forearm exploded in goosebumps.

The murder of crows' squawking swelled. The birds danced about, scooting one way and then another, flapping their wings wildly. They craned forward to better see the moment where a workplace romance could very well begin.

Feeling self-conscious, Lois snatched her hand from David's grip. Before she knew it, she was backing out of her parking space while a dejected David offered her a little departing wave.

The murder continued their song until Lois was a quarter of a mile away.

The workplace memo announced that the crows had become an epidemic. An exterminator had been called, but in the meantime, Sharpe Athletics associates should proceed with caution as some of the crows were exhibiting aggressive behavior, chasing associates through the parking lot and cawing in a hostile manner if anyone got too close.

The crows lined the five-story building, a living velvet trim, black as night and loud as a fire alarm constantly alerting everyone in the vicinity of an emergency. The associates of Sharpe Athletics were lucky if they left work without a smattering of bird poop decorating their cars. Many called in sick or asked to work from home, but Lois never had an issue. She navigated the murders with ease. The birds seemed to move out of her way as she walked, providing her a wide berth.

Inside the building, she was able to tune out their incessant cawing. And she rather liked looking out the window to see the obsidian down of the crows and the way they blanketed the landscape in black, turbulent life.

Lois's only worry was that Mr. Sharpe would use the crow problem as an excuse to cancel their meeting, which was scheduled for the next day. If he did...well, Lois wasn't sure what she'd do, but if the burning feeling in her chest at the very thought of Mr. Sharpe dismissing her again was any indication, it wouldn't be good. Maybe she'd quit or call him a horrible name, something that would require an intervention by HR. Lois hoped it wouldn't come to that.

One more day.

One more day.

One more day. And I can change the company.

Lois poured her brains and energy into the numbers and figures that chugged Sharpe Athletics ever forward. If she worked hard, she convinced herself, the day would go by faster. She'd leave on time, cook a healthy dinner—perhaps something that involved quinoa—and turn in early. Tomorrow morning, she'd put on her brand new power dress and *make* Mr. Sharpe listen to her. She wouldn't let him cancel again.

A crow landed on the window ledge near Lois's cubicle with a gentle *thud,* its head knocking against the glass. Beady eyes peered in at Lois appraisingly. She offered the bird a waggle of her fingers and a half smile.

A moment later, a second bird appeared on the ledge. And then a third, fourth, fifth, and sixth. Lois's very own murder eyed her through the window, their feathers shimmering, their wings fluttering in a nervous rhythm. Lois stared at them, transfixed by their odd behavior, six crows jammed into such a small space, determined to fit.

Without warning, all six opened their beaks and let forth a series of cries in perfect unison. Strangely, Lois was not startled by the sudden bleating. Rather, she felt drawn to it, mesmerized by the murder outside her window. She pushed her chair back from her desk, stood, and walked over to the glass. The birds did not draw back. They remained flush against the pane, even as Lois stroked the window, longing to be outside, to join them.

"Lo, I have news for you." It was David. Behind her.

The crows disbanded, leaving Lois feeling dreamy, her fingertips chilled from the glass.

"Lo, are you okay?"

Lois jolted out of her avian trance and turned to find a smiling David. She couldn't help but grin back at him, crooked teeth be damned. "What is it?"

"Jerry's totally on board with your algorithm."

David's words slapped Lois in the face. Her feet felt like lead. "Jerry? You mean Mr. Sharpe?"

"Yes," David said, taking a step toward her. The fluorescent light reflected garishly off his perfect hair. "We were just in a meeting. Our financial strategy for the next fiscal year came up, and I told him about your calculation."

Lois was sure she'd transformed into a cold, marble statue. She couldn't move. She felt so heavy.

"I doubt I did it justice or explained it properly," David said, close enough now to reach out and grab Lois's arms. His hands felt like cold, slippery, unforgiving ice. He gave her a little shake. "But I pitched it, and he's all over it. Thinks it'll revolutionize the way we do things."

"*You* proposed *my* algorithm?"

"I gave you all the credit, of course," David said. He looked happy. So happy for her. She tried to feel it, but beneath her skin, the only thing she could feel was rage.

Lois pulled away from David's grasp and ran down the hall toward the southeast building exit. When she reached the door, she pushed it open with enough strength to make it bang against the building exterior.

Outside, the air was electric. Crows circled in low, determined, concentric loops. Their incessant cacophony provided a tumultuous, energetic soundtrack in the afternoon air. Everywhere she looked, Lois saw a flash of black, a ruffle, a shake. A murder.

Lois's footfalls pounded in quick succession as she walked the perimeter of the parking lot. With each step, her blood percolated. Emotions coursed through her rapidly beating heart. She felt fire in her fingertips.

Her sudden rage surprised her. She understood the anger borne from Mr. Sharpe systematically making her feel less than by ignoring her. Her fury toward David was more difficult to process. Sure, he was trying to help. It wasn't his intention to hurt her, she knew that, but it stung nonetheless. It felt like betrayal. And of course, Mr. Sharpe, dasher of dreams, had no issue listening to her idea when it came from *someone else's* mouth. Someone like David.

Halfway around the parking lot, Lois noticed the crows were following her. In an arrowhead formation, they flew through the air above, allowing her to lead them.

Lois was oddly pleased by this discovery. When she made the final curve around the parking lot and started back toward the Sharpe Athletics office, she had a new tenacity in her step. Not to mention a gargantuan murder of crows who literally had her back.

She flung open the door to the office, and the crows followed, swooping inside, invading the space. They cawed excitedly, perched on cubicle walls and rolling chairs, and dove low to torment Lois's coworkers, tousling their hair and pecking their cheeks.

A core assemblage of crows followed Lois down the long hallway toward Mr. Sharpe's office. Lois ignored the screams, the rapid movements of her coworkers who pushed and stumbled and sprinted for the exits. She had somewhere important to be.

As she turned down a row of cubicles, Lois saw David in the aisle, fear in his eyes, tension in his stance. He radiated pure adrenaline. "Lo," he managed and then dove into a nearby cube to take cover.

For once, Lois ignored him.

Finally, she reached her destination won. She threw open Mr. Sharpe's office door, strode in, and sat down in a chair. Before Mr. Sharpe could react to her abrupt arrival, a collection of crows flew into the small space in rapid succession. Cooperatively, they circled Mr. Sharpe and Lois at a breakneck speed, the wind created by their wings whipping Lois's hair across her face and, more importantly, creating a circular energy field from which there was no escape.

Lois let Mr. Sharpe scream for a few minutes. He batted at the crows, called for help, tried to stumble through the whirling dervish of bird bodies, only to be pecked and prodded and bumped. Finally, he collapsed into his office chair, exhausted and slipping quickly into a state of shock.

A single crow broke from the pack and landed on Lois's shoulder. The bird nuzzled Lois's cheek, and she smiled. She primly clasped her hands together and leaned forward. "Mr. Sharpe, it's time for you to start listening to me."

At home, when Lois took off her work clothes, she found a solitary black feather tucked between her shirt and her breastbone. She laughed at the discovery and carefully placed the trinket on her desk. It would be a reminder of one of the best days Lois had ever had at work.

She slipped into her most comfortable pajamas and cooked herself a sumptuous dinner of spaghetti and meat sauce. Lois smiled as she ate, thinking of the promise that tomorrow would inevitably bring. She'd been right all along. Tomorrow *would* be a big day.

After dinner, Lois wandered into her bedroom and examined the contents of her closet. She needed to pick out something to wear to work, something special. It would need to demand attention from people like Mr. Sharpe, who had ignored her for far too long.

Something that would flutter when she walked. Something that spoke of her innate power. Something black.

Pursuit

Moments before you register the scrape of shoes on pavement, the air around you grows tight and heavy. The atmosphere coils like a spring, and your heart dances in your chest, missing every other step like a bumbling debutante who isn't ready for the chase despite years of training. No need to look over your shoulder, you know what you'll find. Teeth, looming in the darkness, smiling. Ready to snap. To make a meal of your fear.

You quicken your pace, though you know it won't do you any good. You've been spotted. Tagged. Decided upon. He's coming, whether you're ready or not. Footsteps echo down the street and reverberate through your spine, steady and relentless as a metronome.

In the dark, the houses in this neighborhood are nothing but piles of stucco and wood and brick. You're traversing an abandoned wasteland. An inhospitable place with nowhere to hide, no one to ask for help. You should've let Johnny walk you to your car. He offered, and his smile is bright enough to light up the night, but it seemed like such a hassle to bother him when you only had maybe a quarter of a mile of suburban sidewalk to navigate.

You told him you'd be fine. You were wrong.

Because the thing in the night spotted the dip of your cleavage. Caught a whiff of your honeysuckle shampoo. Heard the click of your boots on the sidewalk.

Or perhaps you were simply in the wrong place at the wrong time.

A cramp lances through your side, because you aren't breathing properly and you're moving too fast and anxiety is rippling through your muscles and where the fuck is your car? You swore you parked closer. Each hulk of metal you pass boasts a license plate that isn't yours. You hate these inert red herrings. They are distracting. They breed false hope.

You know there's only one way to escape. You have to find your silver hatchback before his teeth close about your throat.

Metal pinches your palm as you fumble with your keys, transform your fist into a pointy weapon. This is why keys fit so neatly between fingers, isn't it?

I'll slice and dice you, asshole. Don't come any closer!

You're dying to hit the unlock button on your key fob, but you're afraid it's too soon. You can't unveil your destination until you can taste the exhaust, smell the pine-scented air freshener your dad hung from your rearview mirror the last time he helped change your oil.

Your pursuer's footsteps haven't sped up, and yet, he's right behind you. A snarl rips through the bushes nearby, and you croak—a weak, pathetic sound. There's a chuckle and then rabid panting, hot and excited, like that of an overenthusiastic lover. Musk tunnels through your nose, down your throat, turns sour in your stomach. He's reaching out to grab your hair. It's so easy to pull...

But you're at your car and the ugly scratch where that lady sideswiped you two weeks ago suddenly looks like salvation. Your car lights pulse as you unlock the door, and a tear slides down your cheek. You know this isn't the end. Nothing is guaranteed, but now you have a chance.

You wrench open the door and throw your body into the driver's seat. *Slam. Click.* And then...stillness.

You count to five.

Breathing shakily, you look in your rearview, then over your shoulder. The backseat is empty. The windshield frames a quiet, undisturbed street lit up periodically by slices of butter-colored light. You melt into the seat and stare into sweet nothingness.

Your fingers drift to your neck, still sticky from his breath. Tooth-shaped indentations decorate your skin. As you run your fingertips over the grooves, you imagine a petal-pink constellation pulsing right above your jugular.

That was close, but you made it. You're safe. You're—

Nearby, a woman screams. Teeth gnash in the night.

You pray for morning.

The Girl Who Lost Herself

Once upon a time, there was a girl who could turn into whatever others wanted of her.

She first discovered this power as a child during a shopping trip with her mother. In a department store fitting room, the woman muttered something about her daughter eating too heartily. The snaps on a pair of discount jeans simply wouldn't close over the girl's belly. Fingernails and metal embellishments pinched the child's skin as her mother struggled with the closures. "I wish you were smaller."

And then she was.

The girl's mother looked on in wonder. The pants fit perfectly now. Her little one must have been pulling a prank, she reasoned. Sticking out her stomach on purpose.

The girl, however, had not been playing a game. She'd experienced a physical change. The air had scooped out a piece of her and banished it into the ether. Her instinct was to cry. To scream that something was wrong. But happiness had replaced the irritation on her mother's face, and so, the little girl thought perhaps this was a good thing. She went home with not one but three pairs of new pants that day.

As the years passed, the girl discovered that her physical transformations were only possible if someone wished her to change aloud *and* she also desired the change herself.

At the county fair, her father said he wished she were a touch taller so they could ride a rollercoaster together. The girl grew. Her father beamed. Their smiles twinkled in the night as they pulled the metal safety bar across their waists.

In high school, the girl's first boyfriend mentioned that he wished she had bigger breasts. She experimented with her body in front of the mirror that night, watching her nipples rise and fall until she was satisfied with the results. A week later, she lost her virginity, which she didn't particularly like, but her boyfriend was happy, so she was, too.

In college, the girl met a man she thought she really liked through a dating app. She bought a fake ID so they could meet in person at a bar. He was handsome and funny, and after three beers, the girl decided she wanted to keep him forever.

In his apartment, she kissed him hard and pulled him into the bedroom. Clothes discarded, she straddled him. "I have a secret," she whispered as the man squeezed her hips. "I can be whatever you want me to be."

The man laughed. He reached up for her, but the girl caught his wrists. "I'm not joking."

Despite the beauty suspended above him, the man wondered momentarily if bringing someone so young and inexperienced back to his place had been a good idea. Coeds were eager to please, but they could also be a little intense.

"You like blonds, right?" the girl asked. "I remember you said that in your profile."

The man hesitated. He did, but he wasn't about to tell the naked girl sitting atop him with chestnut hair cascading in gentle waves over her creamy, white shoulders, that he wanted something different.

"I like brunettes, too," he said.

The girl pouted. Rolled her deep blue eyes. "I'm trying to show you something. Just say that you wish I was blond."

"Fine, I wish you were blond."

The girl's hair color changed, quick as a flash. Where there were once dark tresses, there were now honey-colored locks.

The man was stunned. He fell limp against the mattress, wishing to sink into it, but he had nowhere else to go. He stared up at the girl, aghast.

The girl giggled and shook her head, tossing her blond mane to and fro.

"How?" the man asked.

The girl shrugged, then dove for his lips.

The next night, the girl showed up for their date with her blond hair aglow. Her trick had resulted in such ardent lovemaking the night before, she decided to keep the new trait. She wanted to please this man. To keep him happy.

After dinner, the couple again retired to the man's apartment for late-night kisses and mischief. "What do you want tonight?" the girl asked.

The man thought about simply saying "you," but based on the previous night's pouting, he doubted the girl would accept this as a suitable answer.

"Purple hair," he said.

The girl's hair changed into a vibrant shade befitting royalty. He told her she looked like a queen, and she rewarded him by biting his neck. Just when he thought they were done talking for the evening, the girl pulled away. She rose from the bed, standing nude in the middle of his room.

"I can do so much more," she said. "Who's your celebrity crush?"

The man was worried that this was a trap, so he remained silent. The girl crawled onto the bed, poking his limbs. "You're scared," she whispered. "You don't have the guts to tell me what you want."

The girl pinched and prodded until a name fell from the man's lips. He waited for the girl to storm out of his room. The pop star he'd named was the lead singer of a Korean girl group and looked nothing like his young coed.

The girl's eyes sparkled in the dim, then transformed, deep brown replacing their natural blue. The girl shrunk three inches. Her long hair shortened into a fashionable black bob. Bones shortened, lips thinned, and skin rippled as it succumbed to a different hue.

The man couldn't believe his eyes. A perfect copy of Chae-Won stood in his bedroom, smiling at him seductively.

As he stared at this impossibility before him, his gut torqued. It was an unpleasant sensation—and more than that, it was the first of many warnings—but the hot blood pumping through the man's veins eclipsed his discomfort.

That night, the man partook in a fantasy.

And the girl, she had her man.

A few weeks later, the girl stopped going to her classes. Education felt like a laughable ambition in light of her natural ability to shift. Shifting allowed her to please, and pleasing allowed her to fit in wherever she chose. She chose to be in the man's musty apartment, where they could explore the depths of her talents and his desires.

The couple dove headlong into an easy routine of excess and casual theft. Each night, the girl arrived at the man's door dressed as the previous night's fantasy. She'd ask him what he wanted, and he'd pick a new type of woman to sleep with. They'd fall into bed, all teeth and tangled desires and want, want, want.

During their trysts, the girl shrugged on the skins of so many others—an MMA fighter; a Black actress they both watched on a popular sitcom; a ballerina; an Irish lass with milky skin, red hair, and freckles; an Indigenous woman; an approximation of Cleopatra; a swimsuit model; a mermaid (which proved a strange sexual experience for both, but in the end, they could say they tried it).

The girl loved the wonder and joy she saw in the man's eyes as she became something other than herself. His excitement fueled her self-confidence, and she rode the sensation until they were rumpled and exhausted from lovemaking. She'd kiss him in the afterglow and think, *This is it, this is all that I want.*

But inevitably, her high would break. She would slip into the bathroom to clean up and melt back into her original form. It wasn't an easy process. She had to reconstruct her body from memory, and all too often, she couldn't recall the exact location of that mole on her arm, the degree of curvature of her neck, or the texture of her skin.

At the end of each night, she was a little different than she'd been the day before. The only immutable constants were the sad, tired nature of her eyes reflected in glass and an unshakable heaviness in her chest. The girl was quick to blame her tired eyes on long nights with her man and the weight on her heart as indigestion.

Her man was happy. Nothing else mattered.

The man watched the girl return from the bathroom each night, visibly deflated and increasingly fragile. Ever paler and thinner, as if she was sinking into herself. When she nestled into the C-shaped space between his neck and knees, he imagined holding a shell against his chest. Every night, the man asked if the girl was okay, and every night, she gave him the same response: "What we did was magic. I'm great."

And so, the couple routinely fell asleep feeling deeply sated and deeply uncomfortable. The man's guts continued to twist. The burden on the girl's heart grew heavier and heavier. Neither spoke a word to the other about what they felt or what they did or how they'd both developed a disconcerting feeling that the ways in which they were using the girl's magic were wrong and destructive and dangerous.

One night, as she climaxed, the girl felt a great tear in her chest. She saw white and collapsed atop the man, who misread her fainting for ecstasy. He held her close, unaware of what had broken inside her.

When the girl came to, she was drenched in sweat, cradled in the man's arms. After a few deep breaths and no further episodes, the girl excused herself to the bathroom. For once, she was desperate to return to her own skin.

Little did the girl know the explosion in her chest had been her magic sputtering out. Though she attempted to conjure the color of her hair (was it coffee or chocolate?), the shape of her cheekbones (sharp or rounded?), and the length of her toes (was it the second or third that was longer than the rest?), her body refused her whims.

She could not remember herself, and instead, a carousel of the identities she'd assumed spun brazenly around her brain. The girl closed her eyes tight. She tried to banish the images of the women she'd conjured and put on as casually as a glove, but they had no interest in leaving her be. The women demanded to be seen.

And just as she had taken from them, they took and took and took from her.

When she opened her eyes, the girl had no hair, no skin, no lips. Everywhere she looked she saw nothing but bone. She wanted to scream, but possessed no lungs to trap or expel air. She wanted to cry, but lacked the tear ducts necessary to do so.

She wanted to blink away the image in the mirror, but she had no eyelids to mask the atrocity of what she'd become.

The girl exited the bathroom. Her bones clinked and clanked as she made her way back to bed. She hoped the bond they'd formed was enough. That she'd given enough of herself to him.

She prayed the man would accept her now, forever naked before him, unable to be anyone but herself.

Heartless

It begins so early,
The carving,
The bloody separation.
The lessons that little girls are supposed to be nice,
To love everyone,
To give of themselves.

So, in kindergarten classrooms, we crack open our bird-
chests
And use the sharp edge of a cardboard valentine
To scrape out a sliver of what's inside.
Our crushes toss out the bloody cards we give them,
And consume heart-shaped candy
As the cast-aside bits of our anatomical hearts
Stop beating,
Buried beneath half-chewed gum and cellophane
wrappers
In plastic trash receptacles.

We don't notice it then,
The absence,
Because the sacrifices are small,
And we aren't yet taught that your heart
Doesn't grow back.

In grade school, we're boy-and-girl crazy.
We tear out chunks of our hearts
And proudly display them in our diaries.
We discard our last names and replace them with the
Sir-names of the boys and girls we like.
We smudge our secrets with blood
And heart matter,
Thinking that if we write our fantasies down
They will come true.

We give up more of ourselves at this tender age,
But we don't feel the pain yet.
We're the ones doing the pulling, the prodding,
And we only skim the surface of our hearts,
Only whittle away at the outermost layer,
So it's a small sacrifice.
Our hearts continue to thrum
Strong and resilient
And protected by bone.

We learn about heartbreak in high school,
When we fumble with feelings
And zippers

And bra hooks
And reclining car seats.
We give larger,
More vital,
More precious
Parts of ourselves,
Hips and legs and lips and throats.
And we think that the wild beating
Inside our ribcage is a sign
That our hearts want to escape.
To be offered to another in full.
We try to pull the whole organ
From our chest
But it's hard to separate all the
Sinew and muscle.

We offer up what we can,
Performing impromptu vivisections,
Smiles on our faces,
Fingers dripping gore,
Hoping that boy,
That girl,
That dream,
Will press our half-slaughtered hearts to their chest
With tender reverence.

We hope they'll see what we've done
And feel the urge to reciprocate,
To reach within their own chests,

Carve up their hearts, and help us fill that empty space
That's been accumulating,
Because we give
And give
And give.

Sometimes, we're rewarded,
And at home in our bedrooms,
We connect a piece of our beloved's heart
With our own
Using a fish hook and the finest thread.

Other times
They just aren't ready,
And we're left with a gaping hole
Where blood and life and promise
Once hung.

In college, we meet the tricksters.
They give us beautifully wrapped boxes,
Which they claim contain their hearts,
Pulsing and alive and just for us,
But all too often, the boxes
Are empty,
Or filled with something that is trying too hard
To be a heart, but in fact,
Is not.

We hold out hope.

We continue to give
And to collect.
We accept all the gift boxes
Until they fill our dorm rooms with empty promises,
Because someday—
Since we've given so much of ourselves,
Since we were sweet
And generous
And gave them bloody strips of our very essence—
They must feel compelled to give us something real,
right?

We say,
Please, my love,
Become a part of this body.
My body.
Our body.

We feel the pain now,
The pinch of a phantom ventricle,
Absence stinging like so many papercuts,
Our mangled hearts struggling to beat,
Struggling to keep us alive.
We're patchwork dolls,
Our mis-matched hearts a map of where we've been,
Who we've loved,
And how many have left us behind.

Be patient, they say.

Giving and not receiving is all part of the process.
Someone will be ready to give you their heart
Someday.

And so we become our own doctors,
Repairing tears and scissoring tissue and prescribing
therapy
Found at the bottom of wine bottles
Or on dancefloors with partners who disguise
The smell of disappointment with perfume or cologne.
We do yoga,
Thinking a cosmic shift in energy will restore
That which has been lost.
We talk to friends, who share similar woes
But also their successes,
And these stories keep us focused,
Keep us moving forward.

We marvel at our ability to adapt,
To survive
Despite the constant carving.

Every so often, we dig curious fingers into our skin
And pull back muscle and bone.
We take inventory
To better understand how much we've given away
And what we have left.

As we gaze in the mirror

And watch our scarred, disfigured muscles pulse,
We know we can't do this forever,
Can't continue to make offerings
Without receiving more in return.

Though our reserves feel endless at times,
They are finite.

And what could be worse than finally finding someone
Who deserves your heart
And holds their own out to you with bloody, able fingers,
Only for you to find your chest empty,
Picked clean by undeserving lovers
Who took so much from you,
Knowing they themselves were heartless all along?

Extraction

Val's face is a goddamned minefield. Her skin, magnified twenty times over and laid bare beneath the glow of harsh LEDs, spills its dirty secrets across the glass. Inflamed, raised bumps. Gaping pores—needy, eager, and ever ready to swallow grime and filth and bacteria. Val imagines the network of trapped oil, dead skin cells, and debris snaking through her face. Her imperfections have always run deep.

Flawed skin has been Val's nemesis since she began puberty at age eleven. Seemingly overnight, a barrage of pimples sprouted across her chin, cheeks, nose, and forehead. Her mother took her to the store, where they bought facial cleanser, toner, and oil-blotting tissues. Val used them religiously, but her face remained mottled and craterous. She learned how to pop pimples safely and experienced great satisfaction watching the grime exit her face in snaking strings or powerful explosions—but the blemishes always returned. Even an appointment with a dermatologist during which he popped every pimple on her face with a fine needle proved a fruitless pursuit.

Thank God for skincare products. Because there's always something new to try, the beauty industry has proved a buoy in the storm for Val over the past twenty years. Behind every advertisement for skin creams and purifying masks and spa treatments, she finds hope. Val will exhaust every option available to her in the quest for true beauty. It's only a matter of time until the puzzle pieces click into place, she discovers the correct regimen, and her perseverance is rewarded with dewy, silky, uninfected skin.

But tonight, Val feels the weight of defeat looming above her like an anvil. Self-loathing burns deep and hot in her gut, and tears threaten to stain her cheeks.

It's time.

Heart racing, she plucks a silver package from the bottom drawer of her vanity. The face mask packaging is mundane, but Val is well aware its contents are anything but ordinary. ClearOut face masks are powerful—so powerful they were banned within three weeks of their debut. Val blames their quick departure on a combination of user error and a marketing team who decided to advertise ClearOut to *everyone* when it obviously only should have been promoted to the beauty elite—that dedicated one percent who will go to great lengths for perfection. Everyday consumers weren't ready for such a potent formula. They didn't respect the product. Got themselves into trouble.

But Val isn't like them. She has a deep reverence for beauty products and understands the slavish sacrifices you have to make in the name of self-improvement. For example, she bought this face mask on the dark web and paid twenty times its retail price.

She would've gladly forked over enough cash for ten ClearOut masks, but the dealer only had the one.

This one. The only chance Val will ever have to experience its awesome power.

She rips open the sleeve and peers inside. Val's seen countless ClearOut videos made by beauty vloggers and influencers. She knows what to expect, and yet, disappointment flares in her chest. The mask is white, surrounded by clear, citrus-scented sludge. It's so...pedestrian. She wishes its appearance was a little more impressive. More indicative of the magic it's rumored to contain.

It doesn't matter what it looks like, Val thinks. *It just needs to work.*

Despite her pep talk, apathy about the ClearOut mask's lackluster appearance continues to sit heavy in her chest. And that won't do. Val knows you must approach every treatment with optimism in your heart. You have to *believe* it will work. Imbue the essential oils and chemical concoctions with a hearty dose of positivity. *You* are an important part of the solution.

Besides, negativity, stress, and frowning breed wrinkles. Wrinkles are counterproductive.

Val closes her eyes, inhales the soothing aroma of the face mask, and goes to her happy place. A movie reel spins to life in her brain. She watches a montage of women trying to remove ClearOut masks, their skin stretching away from their cheekbones, refusing to release the swatch of fabric. Their faces are red with effort, gleaming. Their jeweled acrylics claw wildly. One woman manages to rip off a piece of the mask, and the movie pauses. The camera zooms in on the woman's skin, pink with irritation, but also tight, smooth, and clean.

Val smiles as her pulse kicks into high gear. Blood rushes to her face, and fresh resolve fills her limbs. These videos are proof that ClearOut masks work. Maybe there's a little pain to contend with, but it's a small price to pay in the grander scheme of things. The women in the videos couldn't see past their momentary discomfort, but Val can.

When the time comes to remove her mask, Val won't panic or call for medical assistance or complain on social media about ClearOut when all it did was fulfill its promise. Her experience will not be punctuated by screams. It will be liberating. Holy. She'll relish the sensation of every extraction.

The mask is cold and slippery, reminiscent of a dead animal left out in the rain. Val reads the instructions three times—just in case—then uses her fingertips to unfold the material and press it firmly against her skin. She envisions the gel seeping into her bloated pores and swallowing all the junk her face harbors. A small moan escapes her lips.

And now there's nothing left to do but wait. As much as she wants to watch this face mask do its thing, Val knows that if she remains standing here in front of the mirror, fifteen minutes will feel like fifteen hours. She needs distraction or the anticipation will eat her whole.

Val sets an alarm on her phone and crawls into bed. A podcast will keep her company for a bit. And then, it will be time to re-emerge, fresh-faced and glowing.

When Val wakes, her phone is silent and her eyes are crusted with sleep. She grabs her device and looks at the time. It's the middle of the night, hours since she applied the ClearOut face mask. She pokes at her screen and realizes she set her alarm for AM instead of PM.

It's only then that Val registers intense discomfort. It's the sensation of pulling your hair back too tightly in a ponytail, taxing your scalp, testing its pliability. Except this sensation is centered in the middle of her face, as if someone has grabbed a hunk of her skin and pulled it away from her bones. The image of a shrunken head lights up her brain as Val scrambles out of bed and into her bathroom.

Her heart drops to her feet when she flicks on the light. The ClearOut mask has fused to her face. She can't delineate between the place where the white material of the mask ends and her caramel-colored skin begins. Her fingertips rove, grasping for purchase, but to no avail.

I'll have to dig. The thought is gruesome and white-hot and unhelpful.

Val turns on the tap and splashes her face with water, hoping the saturation will loosen the mask, but ClearOut is like a goddamn shield. Not a single drop breaches the barrier. There is zero absorption.

Adrenaline rattles though Val's limbs, rendering her movements shaky. She grips the counter to still her trembling hands and leans forward toward her reflection. The skin surrounding the ClearOut mask is stretched within an inch of its life. Val can see the delicate system of her veins pulsing below.

She takes a deep breath and closes her eyes. She remembers the promise she made to herself, that she wouldn't descend into hysteria, no matter what. Yes, this situation is less than ideal, but she can figure it out. She will persevere, because she is strong and capable and has battled bullshit skin for years, the scariest opponent of all. She will be fine.

Val takes a pair of tweezers out of a drawer. She leans into the mirror, tilts her head back, and finds a seam at the bottom of her cheek. This is a good place to begin. If the skin becomes irritated in this area, it'll be easy to hide. Val's coverup is the best money can buy. She also owns a horde of stylish turtleneck sweaters.

She prods gently at first, sure the edge of the mask simply needs a little encouragement to come free. Two minutes later, Val's muscles burn with effort, and she hasn't made any progress. She attacks a new area between her forehead and hairline with the same result.

I'll have to dig. That troublesome thought is back, and this time, Val accepts that it may be true.

She soaks a cotton ball with alcohol and rubs vigorously against her cheek parallel to her ear. She douses the tips of the tweezers to disinfect them. A skin infection is the last thing she needs.

A trickle of blood snakes down Val's face as she makes the first puncture. The sight is so startling, she drops the tool into the sink. She swears, scoops up the tweezers, and drenches them in alcohol a second time.

Get it together. No pain, no gain.

Val inserts the tip of the tweezers into the divot she's created in her skin, presses the pincers together, and pulls. The pain is immediate, sharp and unforgiving, but Val concentrates on her reflection. She's snagged the edge of the mask. She's getting somewhere.

Val pauses and lets the pain dissipate a bit before counting down from five and giving the mask a sharp tug. She hears a disconcerting ripping sound, and then all she can see is red. The side of the mask has pulled free, but it's taken Val's skin with it. Agony courses through her, and she stumbles backward, the tweezers falling from her hand. Her shoulders meet the wall and she slides down to the floor. The faux-marble tiles are spattered with crimson flecks.

What the fuck have I done? A tear careens down Val's cheek and seeps into the open wound. She wails and kicks her legs, then punches the floor until she can feel her pulse in her knuckles. Anything to dampen the pain.

Val's heart pounds hard against her ribs, and she knows she needs to get her body under control. Dying of a heart attack in her thirties would be too damn tragic.

She closes her eyes and cues up her mind-movie, but her brain automatically pulls the most recent film reel. Images of women trying in vain to pull face masks from their faces splash against her consciousness. Not helpful. Val needs to switch the feed.

She screws up her face (as much as she can) and concentrates, trying to remember the last time she was truly at peace. The new film clicks into place.

Val is floating in a bubble bath. The room smells like sandalwood thanks to a lit candle balancing on the lip of the tub.

Instrumental music pours from her phone, the kind of reedy, crystalline sounds you expect to hear in a meditation circle.

This reverie steadies Val, calms her down. Her heart slows from a full-out sprint to a light jog. When she feels like she's back in control, she climbs to her feet and looks in the mirror. Her face is grotesque, pulled taut around the periphery, bludgeoned on her right cheek. She's a walking nightmare. She needs help.

Val is about to go into her bedroom to retrieve her phone and call 9-1-1 when she sees something bright and wavy in her reflection. She blinks hard, convinced she's hallucinating, a response to pain and shock, but the undulating motion continues. Her curiosity flairs. Val's blood is drunk on adrenaline, and the pain in her cheek has downgraded to a dull throb, so she thinks she'll be okay long enough to investigate this new development. Besides, this information could be helpful for the paramedics when they arrive, right?

She presses her hips into the countertop and hinges forward. The flutter of movement comes from the place on her cheek where she's ripped the skin from bone and muscle. Little yellow tentacles wriggle in the light, as if searching blindly for something to grasp onto.

What the hell are those?

Something unnatural. Alarming. Alive.

Val needs to look underneath the loose flap of skin. No longer worried about staving off infection, she uses her fingertips to peel back her blood-stained flesh.

She gasps. The underside of the flap is teeming with familiar yellow threads. Val has seen them before, thousands of times, but always on the *outside* of her skin after squeezing and prodding and coaxing them up out of her clogged pores. She's a witness to her imperfections—the pus and shit and dirt that's called her skin home for as long as she can remember.

Val watches the yellow bodies squirm. Out in the open, they have nothing to latch onto. Nothing to burrow into. They are vanquished.

She's found the source—and the solution.

"It works," Val says. She laughs, but she can only get a chuckle out before the ClearOut mask pulls at her mouth, reminding her that she is under its control. She closes her eyes, thanks the mask for its miraculous properties, and prays she has the strength to see this final stage through.

She pinches the loose skin on her cheek between her thumb and forefinger, the way she would an extra-sticky piece of tape on a box, and pulls. Val screams as her skin comes free—but not because the pain is exquisite in its malice or because steaming viscera paints her bathroom with the frenetic energy of a Jackson Pollock. She screams in ecstasy. She feels the sweet release of years and years of accumulated gunk exiting her body. The blood that pours forth is a baptism. An ascension.

Val pulls and pulls and pulls until her bathroom floor is littered with skin replete with writhing yellow tendrils. She's out of breath when the final piece of the ClearOut mask comes free. She takes a moment to gather herself before looking in the mirror. When she does, tears prick her eyes.

Not a single yellow flag waves to her from her face. All she sees is slick, pink, pulsing muscle and tissue. White bone peeps out periodically like a nervous toddler hiding behind its mother's strong legs. Everything is as it should be.

Finally, she's beautiful.

My Love, In Pieces

Cell phones were never allowed in the drop-off line at Bailey and Emily's school because, as the other parents were quick to say, they held everything up. I knew this, so I nearly ignored the ringing of my phone, but there was something so out-of-place about a call before eight. Sure, you regularly sent me text messages wishing me a good day or letting me know I'd forgotten my coffee on the kitchen counter, but you rarely *called*.

You only called if something was wrong, which is why I broke the rules and reached for my phone.

But it wasn't you. I didn't recognize the number.

Grasping for a safe, mundane explanation, I convinced myself that it was one of our Japanese investors with an urgent business matter. But that didn't make sense. The number had a local area code, and the hour wasn't optimal for business in Japan.

Unease slithered into my gut as I hit the answer button. As it turns out, reasonably so.

It was a medical admin at Madison County who was trying to reach me. In a raspy voice, undoubtedly the byproduct of years and years of chain smoking, the woman told me there'd been an accident. You'd been admitted to the ICU, and I should come quickly.

In slow motion, the bottom of the world fell out from under me. My stomach flip-flopped and my blood ran cold in spite of the car heater belching out stale, warm air.

Bailey and Emily were carrying on in the back, completely unaware of my sudden concern, singing along to a YouTube video. No doubt you'd have scolded me for supplying them with "brain candy" right before school. But you... you weren't there to reprimand me. You were...

"Wait," I choked, a command directed at both the admin and our girls. I turned in my seat, waved a hand at our pink-clad daughters, and told them to stay put. Daddy would just be a minute.

I yanked the car into park, threw open the door, and stepped out into the bitter cold. It wrapped around me like an icy python, darting into every available crevice, looking to snuff out every ounce of warmth my body held. My teeth chattered as I shut the car door.

A school guard wearing a neon reflective vest approached me, but I growled, literally *growled* at her, which worked. She held up her gloved hands in defeat and trudged away to call out someone else breaking child drop-off protocol.

In a voice barely above a whisper, I asked the admin to repeat everything she'd said. With a patient, practiced voice, she told me your car had succumbed to the ice. It spun out of control and hit an oak tree. You'd suffered a number of injuries on impact, and to help you recover, the doctors had placed you in a medically-induced coma.

I leaned my full weight against the car, my heart racing, my brain spinning. "They did what?"

"It's the safest way for her to recover. You should come to the hospital. We can tell you more when you arrive."

"Of course, of course. I'll be there as soon as I can."

By the time I hung up, I was completely numb from both the relentless cold and the horrific news. In spite of the shock, my innate pragmatism took over. I made two more phone calls, one to Rhonda, asking her to reschedule all of my meetings and calls for the week, and another to Felicity, asking her to watch the girls.

The snarling heat of the car's interior should've been welcome—you always claimed I ran it far too hot—but as I climbed back inside and gripped the steering wheel to steady my nerves, the broiling air felt suffocating.

I cleared my throat and willed my words to come out smoothly and calmly. I couldn't lose it in front of our daughters. "Change of plans, girls. No school today. Instead, you're going to have a fancy tea party and French toast with Aunt Felicity."

As the girls cheered from the back seat, my heart pin-wheeled and I swallowed bile.

I wasn't ready to see you like that, broken and bandaged and so very ashen. Your skin, once the color of fresh cream, was the color of dirty snow. Your face was swollen and bruised, a misshapen piece of fruit, thanks to the airbags. Your leg was broken in two places, but it had been reset and shrouded in plaster. The doctor said one of your lungs had collapsed and you had a concussion. Your injuries were many. Thus, the medically-induced coma. They had you on painkillers and steroids and other medications that had so many syllables, I wondered if the doctor was making them up for my benefit.

The worst part was that wretched plastic tube down your throat, the contraption responsible for your breathing, since you could no longer manage that on your own. I couldn't *see* you. I couldn't see my wife, the shining constant of my life.

My chest grew hot as a branding iron, and I feared I'd spontaneously burst into flame. My flesh would drip from my bones, and then... then, I'd be unrecognizable to you, too. Maybe that would be better.

"She'll wake up, right?" I asked.

The doctor gave me a kind smile. "In time, yes. We'll take her off the barbiturates that keep her under as soon as possible, but she has a lot of healing to do. I can't give you a definite timeframe. Of course, we'll do everything we can to aid in her recovery."

It wasn't the answer I wanted. My fists curled and hardened at my sides, ready to fly, but I held the impulse in. They were just trying to help.

I told the doctor thank you and shook his hand, though my palm was cold and clammy. He left the room, and we were alone.

I sank into a chair, ran my hands through my hair, and listened to the metallic beep of your heart.

It's cliché, but it all felt like a bad dream.

I thought of that morning, of the time before. You'd surprised me, climbing atop my hips in the gray light of dawn, bringing your finger to your lips while grinning mischievously. You'd bit my shoulder to keep from waking the girls. You smiled at me. You gnashed your teeth in the throes of our lovemaking. You were so warm and alive.

A fine pressure mounted in my chest, and I tucked my head between my knees to alleviate a sudden swoon. As I gulped in sour hospital air, an object on the floor near your bed caught my attention. It was blindingly white, slightly round with distinct grooves, no larger than a fingernail.

I lowered myself to the linoleum and crawled toward the object until your hospital bedclothes kissed my shoulders. I held it up to the light.

It was a tooth, an incisor, freshly lost by the look of it.

But how did it get there? Was it yours? Did the doctors knock it out when they inserted your breathing tube?

I hoisted myself up and stared down at you. I rolled the tooth between my fingers. It was like holding a piece of a puzzle but not knowing if it fit anywhere.

Of course, I had to know.

The action felt unclean, treacherous even, but ever so gently, I curled your lip up toward the ceiling. And there, along the top gum line, I found it, the absence of you.

I started toward the corridor, ready to alert a nurse to my discovery, but I paused at the threshold. I looked at you, sleeping, shattered, soundless, and decided you'd been through enough for one day. I didn't want them touching and examining you again. I wanted you to rest. I wanted you to come back to me.

And perhaps most importantly, I didn't want them to take this piece of you away from me. I slipped your tooth into the pocket of my woolen coat, sat down, and took your hand in mine.

Felicity's eyes were swollen when I arrived home, and I was afraid she'd told Bailey and Emily what had happened to you.

"I wouldn't do that, Dan," she said. "I told them I've been sick. Plagued with allergies. After I made French toast and turned on the TV, they stopped asking questions."

I made macaroni and cheese for dinner—from the box, with extra butter because we were out of milk—and I told the girls that you'd been in a bad accident, you were asleep, and you needed lots of rest to get better. Bailey asked if you'd become Sleeping Beauty, and that made me smile.

"Kind of," I said gently. Their little faces were confused and half-sad. I could tell they didn't know what to make of the news. "The doctors are using all the magic they can to help Mommy wake up."

"She needs a kiss," Emily said matter-of-factly.

"From a prince," Bailey added, looking sullen and pushing noodles around her plate.

"Well, there aren't too many of those around," I said, before quickly realizing I'd made an inappropriate joke to our very young children.

You were always so much better at these things. You never faltered, never made a mistake.

"Daddy, did you kiss Mommy to try to wake her up?" Emily asked.

I hadn't. I couldn't. I kissed your fingertips, your forehead, your cheek, but there was no getting to your mouth. No way to kiss you properly. I gulped at my wine before answering. "Of course I did, sweetheart."

"It didn't work?"

"No, Em, it didn't." That admission made me feel like a failure.

"Can we visit Mommy?" Bailey asked, her eyes growing wet.

"In a few days, sweetheart. She might wake up by then." I didn't want them to see you yet. I hadn't been ready, so how could they be? I needed more time to prepare our girls. "In the meantime, you don't have to go to school this week."

Bailey gave me a half-smile. "Can I have Oreos?"

And I knew I'd give them all the junk food, the toys, the TV time I could that week. I'd give them every material thing I could manage, because I couldn't give them you.

It was stupid and maudlin of me, but after I tucked in Bailey and Emily, I opened a new bottle of wine, sank down into the coach, and watched our wedding video. I remember balking at the cost and making comments about gutted bank accounts while you rolled your eyes at me. In the end, I've never regretted forking over the cash for it.

I've always loved that video so damned much, because I've never seen you smile like you did on our wedding day. It's like you were filled with light. Busting at the seams with happiness. Every moment that was captured that day, whether on film or video, featured you grinning like a love-struck idiot, and it made me extraordinarily happy. The thought that I could make you feel that way, it was second to none.

Before I knew it, the bottle of merlot was empty and our decorative pillows, the ones you picked out, were dark and wet. The video came to an end, the screen went dark, and I was swallowed by nighttime silence.

Stumbling upstairs to our bedroom seemed a terrible idea, and climbing into bed without you beside me would be impossible. I decided to sleep on the couch.

I took off my coat and draped it over our recliner. I slipped off my loafers and set my glasses on the end table. I'd be sleeping in the clothes I'd worn that day, but I couldn't care less.

I bundled up under the blanket your mother crocheted us for Christmas last year and tried to get comfortable. My body lazed and calmed, but my mind could not be quieted. The room spun. My mouth went dry. A new round of tears threatened to fall. Consumed by the easy darkness of the living room, I'd never felt so alone.

But then I remembered.

I was up like a shot, groping about in the dim. The moment my hand dipped into my coat pocket, I felt better. More steady. Less manic.

Your tooth felt cool in my palm. It glowed in the shadows, a brilliant fragment of you, and I know it sounds crazy, but it felt like you were there. Perhaps on some other plane of reality, you were. Or maybe you hovered over me like an angel or a ghost—though I didn't really like those comparisons.

For the first time since that morning, I felt like everything was going to be okay. I settled back into the couch, rolling bone between my fingers, until I fell into a deep sleep and dreamed of your smile at our wedding.

I woke to two sets of small hands tugging at my clothes. I fluttered my eyelids open, and two blurry balls of energy danced before me. My head ached, and my body felt pinched and cramped. I groaned a little, and the girls laughed.

"You sleeped on the couch?" Bailey asked incredulously.

"I did."

"And you lost a tooth," Emily said. She was holding my hand, and there in my palm, your tooth twinkled in the morning light. I closed my hand and jerked to a sitting position. My brain swirled and scrambled as a hangover pressed against my temples. Emily pried at my hand, thinking it a game. I kept my fist tight and fished for an explanation.

"It's Mommy's tooth," I began, and it was the wrong way to start.

Emily's eyes widened and she crumpled to the carpet, wailing. In support of her twin, Bailey followed suit. Their harrowing cries exacerbated the pounding in my head, but that pain was nothing compared to my shame. What had I done?

I'd scarred our children for life, that's what. Not twenty-four hours after breaking the news to them that their mother was in a coma, I'd shown them one of her extracted teeth. I was sure a child psychologist would have a field day with this.

"Girls, girls," I said softly. "The doctors taking care of Mommy gave me this..."

I'm such a liar.

"This way it doesn't get lost. I can keep it safe."

The crying continued, the girls inconsolable, and I had no idea what they were thinking. I grasped desperately for some semblance of an explanation they would understand.

I took a breath and tried again. "We don't want the tooth to get lost, because then the Tooth Fairy won't be able to give Mommy her prize."

Bailey's cries softened, and she turned her big green eyes up at me. "The... the... the..." she said between sniffles, "Tooth Fairy? She's coming?"

I scooted off the couch to sit on the floor. I smoothed Bailey's hair back. Emily continued to whimper, but I knew if I could soothe one of them, there was a good chance I could calm the other. "Of course, honey. The Tooth Fairy always comes, when anyone loses a tooth."

"But Mommy isn't here," Emily croaked, and my heart sank to the carpet.

"The Tooth Fairy will still come here, and we can save the prize for when Mommy wakes up and comes home." Of course, I didn't know if you'd ever come back to us.

Oh, the trauma I was inflicting...

But it did the trick. Bailey crawled over and nestled in my arms. A few moments later, Emily joined her. It should have been nice, this family cuddle, but my skin felt slick and oily, and I was clutching your tooth so tightly in my fist, I could feel it biting into the flesh of my palm.

That week, your prognosis remained the same, and our little family fell into a new routine. Felicity came over in the mornings. She made pancakes and poured cereal, did the girls' hair—I'd always been a disaster at that—and, ultimately, kept them as calm and happy as she could. Every day she brought over something new—coloring books, puzzles, movies—and I was filled with such gratitude.

Her presence in our home allowed me the opportunity to be by your side. I was there the moment visiting hours began, and the nurses often had to kick me out of your room when night fell.

I talked to you while you slept. I spent hours recounting the early days of our courtship, how you'd hooked me from the very beginning with your easy smile and boundless energy.

You'd always shined, you know that? And everyone around you became etched in light. Perhaps that's why we all loved you so much. You made us better than we were, more brilliant. Brighter.

Though, in your hospital bed that week, hooked up to gadgets that beeped and snarled, you'd dimmed. Your skin looked like brittle paper, and I could almost see through it. I could trace all your veins, your network of life, though the thought of following that pattern across the whole of your body made me queasy. The bruises on your face bloomed and changed color, from startling purple to lazy green.

Every day, the nurse on duty would say that you'd improved, that she'd seen new color blossom in your cheeks. It was a nice gesture, but I figured they said those things because they were sorry for me, not because you'd gotten any better. I decided they conspired together, because they all said the same thing.

I brushed your hair every day. We watched TV, though I felt guilty that I was forging ahead with the police procedural we usually enjoyed together every week. It was a small thing, but it felt like a betrayal. I decided I'd abstain from watching it the following week. I'd wait for you.

I read you poetry, which you'd always adored and I'd never understood. Nothing changed in that regard.

Except for the night I had to place your tooth under a pillow to satisfy the girls' belief in the Tooth Fairy, I kept it with me always. I'd become increasingly protective of it. It was part of you, and if you woke up—no, *when* you woke up—I knew you'd miss it. Sure, dentists can give you fake teeth, but there's something about having the original *you* intact, isn't there?

And with your tooth at the ready, I'd be the fixer you've always expected me to be. I'd be the one who could put you back together again.

Sometimes, I'd take the tooth out and marvel at it. You'd always had great hygiene, so it was impeccable—strikingly white, though you'd never used whitening toothpaste, completely intact, without so much as a chip or a blemish or a stain.

As long as it was whole, I was able to convince myself that you'd remain whole, too.

And since it never left my side, neither did you.

The bar was dark and dirty and perfect and close enough to the hospital that I didn't feel guilty about going. It smelled like stale beer and bad decisions. Peanut shells crunched beneath my shoes as I made my way to a vinyl stool. The seat had been torn open and duct-taped back together. I could relate. After spending a week watching over you, remaining a steadfast solider by your hospital bed, I was coming apart at the seams. I needed a drink.

I ordered some top-shelf scotch, and the petite bartender, an older woman with bleached-blonde hair and heavy makeup, had to get out a step ladder to reach it. After placing it on the bar top, she swiped dust from the glass.

You always hated it when I drank scotch. You said it made me taste like smoke.

That night, that's how I wanted to feel. Like vapor. Like I could disappear. Because life without you, well, the week had proven that it was all kinds of bullshit.

After I'd downed four glasses of amber-colored liquid in quick succession, the bartender set the bottle on the counter next to me. "You can pour your own, but I'm keeping an eye on you."

I nodded and gave her a bleary wave. The alcohol had begun to lace with my blood. My body grew warm, my fingers tingled, and the edges of the room softened.

I thought I was ready for what would come next.

To tell you the truth, I expected to cry. I longed for it. I wanted to break down in front of strangers and wallow in their pity. I'd orchestrated the whole night, played it out in my mind. I'd go to a bar and share my sob story with any poor schmuck who'd listen. I'd tell them about you, how great you are, and how broken my life had become without you. My tears would earn me sympathy, a free drink, a pity fuck—anything would do.

I never could have predicted that my sorrow would desert me in my hour of need. That white-hot rage would bubble to the surface in its place. That after I finished my sixth glass of scotch, I really wanted to punch something.

The world could keep its condolences. I wanted a wild and violent release. The yearning for destruction snaked down my forearms and through my wrists. The weight of the empty tumbler in my palms felt satisfying and heady. I pushed hard against the glass, wondered how much strength it would take to crack it.

The blonde bartender came over and wordlessly took the bottle away from me, but I didn't care. The alcohol was just a primer, and I'd had plenty. It was doing its job, bringing everything to the surface.

I thought of you then—your jet-black hair and your porcelain skin and your long neck and the way you could make me laugh even when the world was chaotic. I thought of our girls, who'd inherited your dark hair, witty personality, and fear of spiders. I thought of what their lives would be like if you didn't wake up. I thought of the doctors and nurses at the hospital who'd kept telling me all week to be patient and wait and let you rest, and it suddenly seemed like they hadn't been doing *anything* to help.

And then I realized that I might lose you forever.

I pushed back from the bar, growling, sending the vinyl stool tumbling. My arm made a swooping arc and threw something small to the floor. The object skittered and bounced. I stomped over to it and smashed it beneath my shoe. I heard a small, bright pop, and in that moment, it was the sweetest sound I'd ever heard.

Looking back, I have no recollection of reaching into my pocket for your tooth. I just remember the noise it made when I crushed it beneath the heavy sole of my boot.

Not long after, I was unceremoniously kicked out of the bar by a rough-and-tumble bouncer. I went quietly, meaning I didn't fight him. But I guess I wasn't all that quiet, because the tears had finally come. I wailed and blubbered and stumbled through the cold, finally experiencing the rock-bottom release I thought I so desperately needed.

But as I zigzagged across the parking lot, drifting toward drunken incoherence, I recognized that the cost had been too much.

I locked myself in my car, tossed my keys in the back, reclined the driver's seat, and sobbed in confinement. I kept reaching into my pockets, hoping to find another piece of you, hoping what had just happened in the bar had been a fever dream. But, of course, I searched in vain.

In my madness, I'd made sure there would be nothing left of you.

The buzz of my cell phone against my leg woke me the next morning. My eyes flicked open and then demanded to be shut again when bright light barreled into my skull. The vibration in my pocket continued, so with my eyes screwed shut, I rummaged for the device. I brought it close to my face, cracked an eyelid just enough to see the screen for a nanosecond, and hit the answer button. I brought the phone to my ear.

"Hello?" My voice sounded as if I'd gargled with glass.

"Is this Daniel Roberts?"

"It is."

"I'm calling from Madison County Hospital. I have good news. Your wife, Claire, she woke up this morning."

My heartbeat surged. "She's, she's... she's not in a coma anymore?" Heat welled behind my eyelids, urging them open. The morning light was unbearable at first, but I pushed through the pain. My sight was blurry, as if I was underwater. Through the haze, I registered the outline of a steering wheel in front of me. I was in my car.

I groped at the dash, hoping it's true what they say, and old habits die hard. My fingers scrambled this way and that and eventually fell upon the familiar shape of my glasses. I slid them up the bridge of my nose, then blinked wildly. The first thing I saw clearly that morning was a sign proclaiming that this parking spot was for patients only. I was in the hospital lot.

A wave of relief washed over me. I closed my eyes and let my body sink into the leather driver's seat. You'd come back to me, and I was close by. Soon I would gather you in my arms and the world would be right again.

"Yes, Mr. Roberts, your wife is awake." There was something wrong with the woman's voice, even as she shared what was supposed to be happy news. There was a pause on the line, and then the woman's voice again, nervous but firm. "But I'm afraid there's been an incident."

I felt like I'd stuck my finger in a light socket. I jolted upright, and the seatbelt was the only thing that kept me from slamming my chin into the steering wheel. "An incident? What kind of incident?"

"It appears that your wife was attacked last night."

I unbuckled my seatbelt and reached for my woolen coat, which I'd thrown on the passenger seat. When I lifted the material, a fine tinkling sound filled the car. As my eyes lit on the sound's origin, I let out a strangled cry.

Of course, the hospital admin didn't understand. She couldn't see what I saw.

"Mr. Roberts, I promise we're launching a full investigation into the matter."

I flipped the driver side sun visor down and peered into the mirror. My face was speckled with blood.

"Your wife may have been conscious at the time of the attack. We've tried to question her—gently, of course—but she wouldn't stop screaming. We had to give her a mild sedative, for her own safety. She's calmed down, but she keeps repeating your name. We think you being here could really help her. Also, the police are here. You should talk to them."

"Of course," I said, my voice hollow. "Of course. I'll be right there."

I let the phone slip from my fingers.

Shaking, I forced my gaze back to the passenger seat. Medical instruments, silver, sharp, and spattered with blood, reflected the grey light of morning. Strewn among them were small pieces of bone, thirty-one individual fragments in total, all of them extracted from your perfect mouth.

And then, we both were screaming.

This Woman's Work

The change is always excruciating. She screams as her skin stretches, as her bones crack and lengthen and rejoin. No blood is spilled, but she always sees red. The process takes an hour—sixty minutes of endless pain, hollow cries, and a precarious dance with death. Despite the thousands upon thousands of times she's endured the transformation, she's never entirely sure she'll survive it.

Her metamorphosis complete, pain becomes purpose. She leaves her secret den and turns her face up to the moon. As she walks, she wonders if she reached out to touch the silver crescent in the sky, would it burn her fingertips with cold? Or perhaps it would turn out to be a fragile thing and would shatter into shards of stardust at the slightest disturbance. Someday, she tells herself, she'll find out. But tonight, she has work to do.

Despite her size, she's quiet on her feet. Fairytales are wrong about giants. When they traipse across the earth, they don't cause meteoric quakes. What they create is far scarier—shifts in energy, swirls of unknowing that are impossible to escape if you happen to fall into one. Aware of her power, she avoids people and only moves at night.

She carries an hourglass filled with snow-white sand. The item is as light as a single sheet of paper, but it won't be for long. Soon, it will hold incredible weight. It will be difficult to transport home. There will be sweat and scorched muscles and moments when she'll want to give up. But she can't. This is her function. Without her work, the world will fall in on itself, grow sick and sordid and unbearable.

Across the river, she pauses by an old sycamore tree. Knowing radiates through her body. Yes, he's close by. She can feel it like a leech on her skin—a distinct, dirty pull that makes her stomach flutter. He's been hitting things again, anything that gets in his way. People, animals, walls. They all succumb to his fists, because what else can they do?

When she's close enough, she flips the hourglass. As the grains of sand fall, they are no longer white, but flecked with gray and red and black. They buzz like angry bees, throwing themselves against the glass, trying to escape. The woman closes her eyes, letting the hourglass grow heavy in her hands. She takes every-thing from him as he sleeps, dreaming of vitriol and violence.

She's weary when she returns home, but she tamps down her desire to collapse into bed and sleep. Her work is not yet complete.

The change isn't as painful on this end. Shrinking is strange, unnerving and slippery. Her bones go first, sliding out of place and withering back to human proportions. Her skin follows, hanging limp like rubbery slime. For a while, she's simply an excess of stuff, shapeless and immobile. She closes her eyes, practices patience, counts to one hundred over and over again.

When the reversion is complete, she drapes her body in silk and brews a cup of tea. The hourglass opens easily in her hands, and she tips the contents into her cup. The adulterated grains sizzle as they hit the liquid. The drink will taste terrible, like him. Like the brutality that has festered inside his mind, his body, his spirit.

But after so many years, she's grown accustomed to the distaste. She will consume him, swallow down his horrible nature. Within her, it will do no harm. His wickedness will dissipate, snuffed out by something greater than he ever was.

Thanks to her, the man will never swing a fist again. In the morning, his wife will find his skeleton between their cotton sheets. She'll scream, partially out of shock, but mostly out of relief. Because his bones, bleached and useless, will never be as frightening as the monster he was in life.

Seeing Double

Bradley Eaton is going to have sex. And on top of scoring with the hottest girl to ever attend a Kappa kegger—which is a reward unto itself—Anthony DeSilva will finally have to shut his punk-ass mouth and pay up. Bradley's pretty sure the pot's at a hundred fifty dollars now, a small fortune for a college student.

Brad's fingertips brush over the back pocket of his jeans. The condom is still there, thank God. He was afraid it would jostle free while he was dancing or that Anthony would pickpocket it to give him grief and ruin his night.

Brad rarely has the opportunity to rifle in his back pocket for a condom—in fact, this is the same one he's had on hand during every party this semester. Maybe he'll actually get to use it tonight.

The rap music around him throbs with the persistence of a newly stubbed toe. Scantily clad girls walk past him. None of them try to draw his gaze, something that would usually sting, but not tonight.

Brad watches Taylor pump the keg across the room, somehow making the chore appear graceful. *She's* getting *him* a drink. Brad's frat brothers are always going on and on about how you have to lean into the whole male chivalry thing to attract girls. Taylor has turned the tables on him, and he likes it.

Taylor returns holding two Solo cups full of frothy, cheap beer. She grins as she passes one to Brad, their fingers brushing against the plastic. Her dimple flairs in her right cheek.

Goddamn, she's cute. Brad knows she's completely out of his league, which makes this whole scene all the more surreal and satisfying.

Brad especially likes her hair. It's blond, but not that hyper-dyed, platinum shit undergrads gravitate toward. She's a natural blond, her hair the color of light lager and long enough to skim the rims of their beers.

They take their first sip together, eyeing each other over the cups.

"So..." Brad shouts over the music, ready to deliver one of his sure-fire zingers. While eating greasy breakfasts to nurse their hangovers, the men of Kappa share the pickup lines they use on girls at parties. They laugh over the quips that bomb and pocket the ones that lead to make-out sessions—or more. Brad has a doozy planned.

But he loses her before he's able to deliver the line. Taylor breaks eye contact and twists. She pulls her cell phone out of her back pocket. The light from the screen renders her pale and ghostly in the carefully orchestrated dim of the party. Taylor pouts and then replaces her phone.

She leans forward. "Hey, my roommate is having a bit of a crisis. I'm going to the bathroom so I can call her quick, okay?"

Brad's stomach plummets. He squints, trying to discern if Taylor's excuse is legit. Was that really her roommate who'd sent her a text, or is this an arranged exit? It wouldn't be the first time Brad's been ghosted at a party. He thought everything was going so well.

As if sensing Brad's disappointment, Taylor grabs his free hand and brings it to her lips. She slowly licks the length of his pointer finger. Brad's mouth hangs open.

Taylor leans in, and her lips tickle his ear. "I promise I'll be right back."

Brad's pants tighten instinctively. He is still going to have sex. Holy shit, it's definitely still on.

Taylor winks at him before turning and meandering through the crowd of sweaty bodies in the general direction of the Kappa bathroom.

Brad knows she'll have to wait in a long line of collegiate girls with small bladders or smeared eyeliner. And who knows how long her conversation with her roommate will take. Honestly, he doesn't care. Brad will wait all night for this girl if he has to. He's closing this deal if it's the last thing he does.

A seat on the Kappa boys' cheap IKEA couch opens up, and Brad settles in. There isn't anywhere to set down the beers, but he's content to double-fist the drinks, watch the action around him, and wait for Taylor.

At the end of the song, Taylor reappears. She pushes through the crowd, her hungry eyes locked on Brad. When she's close enough, Brad yells, "Hey, that was fast. Seems like you lucked—"

But before he can finish the sentence, Taylor has straddled him, grabbed his face between her palms, and brought her lips to his. Stunned, Brad drops both cups of beer. As Taylor pulls him deeper into their first kiss, he feels cold liquid seeping into his jeans. Brad's sure he's decimated the shitty IKEA couch—but it's a shitty IKEA couch. And his brothers are likely to deem the stains badges of honor when he recounts his night to them.

Taylor ends the kiss, but her body remains pressed close to his. "I missed you."

Brad's game is decidedly unfocused, and he scrambles for a witty response. His brain spins much too fast, hazy with alcohol and lust. What he says next loses any semblance of coolness as it tumbles from his mouth. "Maybe you should miss me more often."

His brothers will laugh at this stupid-as-hell line tomorrow morning, but at least it's an attempt at flirtation. And Brad punctuates it with his million dollar smile, his saving grace. He may not have muscles or designer threads, but his charismatic grin is a weapon.

"I'm staying right here," Taylor says. She smiles wide, but strangely, it's not enough to make her dimple pop again. Or maybe it's just that her cheek is painted in shadow.

"Your roommate okay?"

Why did he ask that? Why didn't he keep the heat going?

It's not all bad, because his faux-concern his will make him appear caring. But he's pretty certain he's just doused their fiery foreplay with a bucket of ice-cold water.

"She's fine. It wasn't a big deal." Taylor flaps a hand dismissively.

"Your roommate said it was a crisis." Why is he pushing this? He blames the beer.

"She blows things way out of proportion." Taylor pushes against his shoulders and stands. She holds out a hand. Of course, he takes it, and Taylor leads him out the front door of the frat house.

Like a goddamn gift, Anthony is close to the front door, surrounded by a gaggle of coeds. Brad locks eyes with his frat brother and inclines his head toward Taylor. Anthony's eyes sweep across the girl appreciatively, and he holds a fist up to his mouth with pride. They bump knuckles as Taylor leads Brad out of the party.

They walk two blocks and pause in front of a blue sedan. "Get in," Taylor whispers, and Brad can't get the passenger door open fast enough. This girl is classy. She doesn't want to do it in a frat house or her own dorm room, probably because of her roommate.

On the other hand, the choice of a car is adventurous and voyeuristic. Brad kind of hopes campus security notices fogged-up windows and an officer raps on the glass. A ticket for indecent exposure would make him a Kappa god.

When the car doors close, Taylor hits the locks, and the resounding click of the doors reinforcing themselves is an unexpected turn-on.

"Brad, I need you to make a very important decision right now," Taylor says.

Brad is practically salivating. This is already one of the most exciting sexual experiences he's ever had, and he has yet to remove a single article of clothing.

"Hey Brad." A familiar voice rings out from the backseat of the car.

Brad jumps. It's Taylor's voice, he's sure of that. But she's also in the driver's seat. It's like this hot girl in front of him is in surround sound.

He twists and peers into the backseat. Taylor's there—the blond hair, the blue flowy shirt, the swash of pink lipstick. She smiles at him.

Brad's gaze flicks back to the driver's seat. Blond hair. Blue shirt. Pink lipstick.

What the hell?

Brad's eyes widen as he connects the dots. "Twins?"

The Taylor in the front seat nods. "Yep, you've been hanging out with both of us tonight."

Brad revisits the events of the evening, which sharpen into focus as adrenaline courses through him.

The text message. The disappearing dimple. They'd switched.

"And now you have to choose," Backseat Taylor says.

"Wait…you're saying…" Brad starts.

"You can only choose one of us, Brad," Front Seat Taylor says.

There's a strange edge to her voice. It isn't husky or playful. Instead, the sound is vaguely threatening. Brad suddenly feels claustrophobic, trapped. He needs some air, a moment to clear his head.

Brad discreetly reaches for the passenger door handle, but it doesn't budge.

"Child locks, Brad," Backseat Taylor says. "We've already come this far. Don't you want to finish?"

Brad catches the sexual innuendo in her words. His primal instincts respond, and heat rushes through him, but he's suddenly feeling a bit nauseated, too. He swallows, and the sound of it in his ears is like a bomb dropping in the quiet of the car.

He really *does* wants campus security to show up right about now. But they're alone. Isolated.

"Uh, can I ask some questions?" Brad asks. He needs to buy time. Figure some shit out.

"Of course," Front Seat Taylor says.

"What are your names? You can't both be Taylor, right?"

"Anna." This response comes from the backseat.

"So, you're Taylor?" Brad asks the girl in the driver's seat.

"Nope. Michelle."

"Neither of you are Taylor."

The girls' blond hair swishes as they shake their heads in unison. They look like dolls and it's creepy as hell, so Brad closes his eyes. He hopes it looks like he's concentrating.

"Okay...who is the engineering major?"

Michelle grips the steering wheel and smiles. "I've got the brains, baby."

"And you're studying...?" Brad asks Anna, peering into the backseat.

"Theater."

Brad nods, as if this information matters.

He decides he needs to ask more pointed questions, to make better sense of what transpired at the party. "This is kind of awkward, but which of you licked my finger?"

Michelle rolls her eyes and her fingernails dig into leather. "Fucking juvenile…" she mutters.

The giggling in the backseat sounds like a babbling brook. "That would be me." Anna waggles her painted fingernails at Brad.

He smiles, but pulls his face into a neutral position when he feels the anger radiating from Michelle beside him.

Brad clears his throat. He directs his next question to the backseat in a lowered voice. "Did you, uh…straddle and kiss me, too?" His question is hopeful. If this girl did both of those things, she's his pick.

Anna's face is masked in shadow in the backseat, but Brad can see her features droop nonetheless.

"That would be me," Michelle says proudly. "And there's more what that came from, Bradley." She purrs his name like it's something sexy.

It's becoming more and more obvious to Brad that he's not going to win here. Sure, maybe he'll get to have sex with a gorgeous girl, but he'll also make an enemy of the sister he doesn't choose.

This whole situation is way too dramatic for his taste. He'd rather go back to the frat house, admit defeat, and suffer the taunting of Anthony than play whatever fucked-up game this is.

"Anna, Michelle, you're both hot and really great," Brad says. "I mean that. I've had a ton of fun with both of you tonight. Which is why I don't think I can choose between you two."

In creepy synchronicity, the girls sigh heavily and sit back in their seats. A cloud of rejection tunnels through the car. Brad thought this magnanimous decision would make him feel better, but it doesn't. He feels like shit. And he can't ignore the fear that continues to gnaw at his neck.

"I'm between a rock and a hard place here—literally." Brad chuckles, trying to lighten the mood with a half-hearted joke about the tightness in his pants, which is still going strong despite the strangeness of this situation.

Brad hears a click and then metal meets his temple. "We didn't want it to come to this, but you have to choose, sweetie."

Another click, and in his peripheral vision, Brad sees the glint of a blade beside him. "Anna's right, Brad. You have to choose." Michelle teases the length of the knife over his thigh. He's absolutely sure that if she feels compelled to, she'll use it.

The knife isn't an empty threat. Neither is the gun trained at his head.

Brad takes a deep breath and then gives the girls his answer.

Bradley Eaton has a system. Every time he sees his girlfriend, Anna, he resorts to screwball hijinks to make her smile. He performs inane dance moves. He tells stupid jokes. He compliments her profusely, waiting for her dimple to pop.

To unknowing bystanders, Brad seems like the most caring boyfriend ever. The truth of the matter is that his endearing performance is entirely self-serving. That dimple is the only way he can tell Anna apart from her twin sister, Michelle, and after *that* Kappa party, Brad isn't taking any chances. Knowing he's with the right twin is the only modicum of control he feels like he has in his relationship, so he holds onto the sliver of power as tightly as he can.

He's terrified of upsetting either of them. Anytime Anna or Michelle look so much as pensive, Brad feels the muzzle of Anna's gun at his temple. He remembers Michelle's knife trained over his thigh. He has nightmares. Brad obsesses over what ifs and myriad disastrous scenarios.

Fueled by fear, Brad has become a consummate listener. He's paranoid, so he's listening for clues in between the lines of normal conversation. He's also become adept at comforting the girls and providing solutions, because fucking hell, if either of them gets upset...well, he doesn't like to think about that. Brad now takes accountability for his actions, even when he isn't in the wrong. He puts out fires before they begin.

Anna showers him with warmth and affection when he's good to her or her twin. Michelle eyes him hungrily, a blunt quality to her gaze that's both tempting and threatening.

Brad often wonders what would have happened if he'd said Michelle's name in the car that night. Would his predicament be identical, or would being with Michelle come with its own unique experiences and consequences? He hopes he never finds out.

Brad is now a Kappa legend, albeit a reluctant one. When Anthony found out he'd been courted by twins at the party and chosen only one of them, he rained dollar bills down on Brad, then sank to his knees and performed a series of ridiculous bows. All of Brad's Kappa brothers are convinced a threesome is imminent, but Brad assures them that isn't the case. He's become very aware that Anna and Michelle don't share well.

But it's not all bad, Brad tells himself. There are perks. Anna's sexual prowess is enough to bring him to his knees.

And it looks like it's going to be one of those nights.

When Brad opens his dorm room door, Anna is there in the dimly lit hallway, dressed in a tan trench coat cinched tight at her waist. It's the middle of summer, so Brad knows there is no practical reason for her to be dressed like this.

Raucous hoots and yells echo down the hallway, but they don't faze Anna. She stares at him, biting her lip.

Brad's roommate claps a hand on his back and says he'll be in the common room studying. His gaze lingers on Anna as he slips out.

"Hi," Brad says dumbly. Being with someone like Anna hasn't improved his game one iota. And when she surprises him like this, it's like he's been hit with a taser and can barely function.

Anna steps into the room, her high heels squishing into the cheap carpet. She locks the door and unties the coat, her back to him. When the fabric hits the floor, all Brad can see is lace and skin and that river of freckles that decorates Anna's hips like splattered paint. She flicks off the lights, pushes Brad onto his bed, and straddles him.

Moonlight pours in from the window, drowning Anna in white light, making her resemble a porcelain doll. Brad reaches up and squeezes one of Anna's breasts...and then realizes he's neglected his system.

His body floods with adrenaline. This is Anna, right? Brad's brain whirs and then he lands on something he knows will make Anna smile.

"You are too damn beautiful." He holds his breath, staring up through the dim, waiting for a response.

When Anna smiles and he sees that spot on her cheek darken, Brad pulls her to him. He tastes her skin, grinds his hips against hers, and flips her over, pinning her wrists above her head. She's wearing black lace gloves, and the patterned material tickles Brad's palms.

Anna is grinning, that spot on her right cheek upgraded to a crater in the shadows, and seeing it fills Brad with relief. Anna squirms playfully beneath him, and the moonlight hits her face just so.

That's when Brad sees that the spot on her cheek isn't actually a dimple. It's a dark dot, something like a beauty mark.

He must be frowning, because Anna asks what's wrong.

"Nothing," Brad says, releasing her wrists. "You've just got something..." He swipes at his own face to mirror hers.

"Oh." Anna licks her gloved finger and rubs at her cheek. The spot dissolves beneath her spit and the rough the texture of her glove. "Look at me, ruining the surprise."

Brad suddenly feels dizzy. She wiped away her dimple. That must mean...

Slowly, the girl beneath him removes her gloves, her eyes trained on Brad. She holds up her naked hands and wiggles her fingers. Brad squints in the darkness, trying to understand what he's supposed to see.

His brain registers the change. Her fair skin is patchy in the moonlight. She's gotten into something that's stained her hands.

"I took care of it. It's just us now."

Brad frowns as the room spins. "You took care of what?"

"Anna," Michelle says. "I've been watching you, Brad. It's crystal clear that you regret the choice you made the night we met. It was supposed to be me, wasn't it, babe?" She sighs through her nose. "Anna just didn't understand. She refused to give you up. I did this for us, so we could have a chance."

Brad's mind starts and shudders, the misfires sending shivers through him.

Is she saying...? Did she...?

Michelle reaches up with blood-stained hands and pulls Brad's mouth to hers. He recognizes the smell of copper and moans, which only makes Michelle hold Brad tighter against her.

Every fiber in his body is telling Brad to push her away.

To run.

To call the cops.

To get the hell out of here.

But every time he musters up the courage to wrench away, Brad feels cool metal press against his thigh. He knows this is likely a figment of his imagination, but...what if it's not? His brain is muddled, and he doesn't know what's real anymore. Is it really a stretch to believe Michelle brought that knife with her, just in case Brad didn't like her surprise?

The only truth he's sure of in this moment is that Michelle is very capable. His new girlfriend knows exactly how to get what she wants—at all costs.

So, Brad doesn't flee.

Instead, he survives.

He kisses the hollow of Michelle's neck. He threads his fingers through hers. He closes his eyes and gives into the darkness, promising he'll never leave.

Forever Longing

She can see it, Christine thinks as she watches a woman with a head of brown curls marvel at her latest piece. *She sees him.*

The customer is standing just inside her tent, chin tilted up, mouth hanging slightly agape as street fair attendees file past. Afternoon light filters lazily through the stained glass suncatcher. A collection of geometric shapes paint the woman's face purple, but it's her awe—pure and childlike—rather than the brilliant color that renders her beautiful.

Christine knows this look. She fingers the crisp bills and smooth coins in the pocket of her sundress, knowing a sale is imminent. She steps closer. "This one is called Forever Longing."

"It's gorgeous. The purple is just...." The woman's fingers reach toward the glass, but they don't make contact. "I've never seen anything like it."

Christine hasn't either. She'd been so startled by the shade of Eric's soul—a deep, dark purple that reminds her of storm clouds—that when it poured forth from her lips, she'd nearly faltered in her process. She'd suppressed a cough, fearing that

Eric's precious life-force would spill from her lungs in a single burst.

She's learned, through trial and error, that if she exhales too quickly, the soul will ricochet off the glass and mist away rather than imbuing it with color. Christine is embarrassed by the number of souls she wasted when she first began working in stained glass—but such is the plight of learning a new trade.

Christine gazes up at Eric's soul, trapped in glass. "It's one of a kind. I'll never be able to recreate that exact shade of purple."

And she won't, because there will never be another person like Eric.

She remembers the way his eyes shined in the low light of the bar. His gaze bore such honesty that night. Christine knew he ached to be touched. Not in a purely sexual way, but rather in a way that inspires deep levels of human connection.

She'd nearly abandoned her scouting mission then, seeing this man's vulnerability laid bare, but then he'd bought her a cocktail, and she realized she was already in too deep. He'd chosen her—and she'd been struck with artistic curiosity.

"It's incredible work," the customer says. She cocks her head to the side. "I'm curious, how do you make stained glass anyway?"

Christine smiles and launches into her regular spiel. It's what customers want to hear, but it's a bold-faced lie, of course. "I use sand, potash—which is an alkali material—and lime to fashion the glass itself." The woman's eyes never leave the suncatcher, even as Christine speaks. "And then combinations of copper oxide, cobalt, chromium, titanium, gold—they give the glass its unique color. After that, I carve the glass. Bring out its shape. Its character."

She and Eric had tumbled out of the bar, clinging to each other in the moonlight. He'd walked Christine to her car, run a finger tenderly over her lips, and leaned in.

Christine had enjoyed the kiss. It was soft and probing and less greedy than she'd anticipated. Eric had moved closer, sealing their bodies together, giving in to her completely. And that's when she took him.

Christine had pressed her fingertips into Eric's shoulders and sucked the air from his lungs. When his chest was empty, she had continued. She moved from collecting air to catching memories and fears and personality traits and dreams. And as she tasted him, she knew he was special. That his soul had such potential.

As she'd worked, drawing him out bit by bit, Christine had imagined how his essence would look, caught in a moment of time, on display for all to see.

"It seems like a lot of work," the customer says.

"You have no idea," Christine says, and she laughs in a casual way that says, yes, creating stained glass is difficult, but it's oh so worth it.

Like all the others before him, Eric had withered into a husk after she'd drained him. He'd been alive, but weak, disoriented, and unable to stand. Christine had eased him to the pavement, given him a kiss on the forehead, and then hurried home to her workshop. She'd been eager to see what Eric really looked like, deep inside, at his very core. She hadn't been disappointed.

"How much for this piece?" the woman asks.

"One hundred dollars," Christine says. She usually charges fifty, but Eric is special. She'll never see purple like this again in her lifetime, and she desires adequate payment to make up for the loss.

The woman doesn't hesitate. She reaches into her designer purse and hands Christine a single bill. Christine plucks the suncatcher from its hook, folds it between sheets of high-quality silver tissue paper, and sets it in a small box filled with bubble wrap. She places the box in a bag, adds one of her business cards, and hands the parcel to the brown-haired woman, who then disappears into the bustle of the street fair.

Christine feels a wisp of Eric's soul thrash around in her chest, and the sensation brings a smile to her lips. The moment he'd kissed her, Christine knew two things: that Eric's soul would make transcendent art and that she couldn't give all of him away. She'd infused enough of his soul into the glass to stain it and then swallowed what was left of him. She'd let him bloom in her lungs. Meld into her. She wanted to feel his naked longing always.

"Forever, Eric," she whispers, pressing a hand to her chest. "Forever."

The Wailing

Elle is mid-sentence when the tooth tumbles from her mouth and skitters across the table. The group to whom she's presenting a new marketing strategy falls silent, and the only noise in the stuffy conference room is bone cartwheeling over glass. Elle watches as the tooth travels toward the center of the table, leaving a trail of spittle and blood in its wake. Finally, it stops. The room is quiet.

Warm liquid drips onto Elle's lip, and she becomes frighteningly aware of the taste of iron. She brings her hand to her mouth. Still gripping the PowerPoint clicker, her knuckle and the device are now tinged red. In disgust and shock, she tosses the clicker onto the boardroom table. As it clatters and rolls, her coworkers push back their chairs, dodging the now-contaminated device.

This is a dream. A crazy, fucked-up dream, Elle reasons as she takes in the horror etched on her coworkers' faces.

Elle closes her eyes, shutting out the boardroom. The befuddled stares. The glaring proof glinting from the center of the table, winking white in the sparse light cast by the projector. She begins to count to five, but she doesn't reach the number. At four, she feels a hand on her shoulder. She prays that she's in bed at home, tucked under her duvet, and this gesture is someone trying to wake her.

But this is faulty logic, because Elle lives alone.

"Elle." The voice is gentle and low. It's her boss, Marjorie. Which means...

No, no, no, no, no, no, no.

"Let's get you out of here."

She tongues the space where her two front teeth should be firmly rooted into her pink gums. The right one is there, strong and immovable, but there's a cavernous gap where the left tooth should be.

A coyote begins wailing in the room—at least, that's what it sounds like to Elle.

Elle hears coyotes crying whenever she visits her friends, who live on the precipice of a gaping canyon. Each night at sunset, a chorus of high-pitched screams weave through the brush surrounding their home. A band of coyotes ensuring none in their pack are left behind.

The coyote call rings in Elle's ears as Marjorie steers her out of the conference room and down the hall to the women's restroom. The sound stops abruptly as Elle crumbles to the tile floor and loses her lunch in the nearest toilet.

Elle drives home with her tooth nestled in a thermos of creamer since there wasn't any fresh milk in the employee refrigerator at work.

"Today is the last day of Dr. Mowry's vacation." The receptionist's high, reedy voice fills the interior of the car. "He'll be back tomorrow, and since this is an emergency, you can come in before business hours. 6am?"

Elle wants to say "Sure" or "That sounds great" or even just a simple "Yes," but her tooth loss has resulted in an embarrassing lisp. In the women's bathroom at work, she'd wailed, "My tooth," but she couldn't manage the "th" sound. The resulting noise was akin to Elle sucking the last of a soda through a straw, a slurping, desperate, empty sound.

The receptionist interprets Elle's hesitation as a desire not to wait. She says, "Your other option is to go to urgent care or the ER. You can get immediate treatment and then call back to schedule a follow-up appointment with Dr. Mowry."

"No," Elle says. She doesn't like the idea of a stranger poking around in her mouth. She's always been head shy; anything to do with the treatment of her eyes, teeth, or ears makes her skin crawl. She's cultivated rapport and trust with Dr. Mowry, so she's not interested in going to anyone but him.

Besides, after some frantic Google research, she doesn't think successful reinsertion of the tooth is possible. A dental implant seems like the best option. She remembers the illustrations of large metal screws drilled deep into a jawbone, topped with fake, new teeth, and shudders. If that's what it takes, full anesthesia will be a must.

"Tomorrow morning is…" She cringes as she lisps and spit flies toward her radio console. "Fine."

At home, Elle dumps the creamer, washes off her tooth, and drops it into a clean glass. The tooth clangs as it falls into the new container, and she flinches, hoping she hasn't chipped or cracked the bone. But then she thinks back to the tooth free-wheeling over the conference table. If it can withstand those gymnastics and refuse to crumble, surely this little bump can't be that traumatic. She fills the glass with fresh milk and places it in the fridge.

She kicks off her heels and goes to the bathroom. Elle pulls her lips back in a silent scream and stares into the mirror. The gap along her top gum is an empty chasm—huge, beckoning, and dark. She imagines being pulled into the blackness. Consumed. Lost.

She shakes her head, and an overwhelming sense of guilt replaces her existential terror. How could this have happened?

Because Elle is squeamish about her teeth, her oral hygiene is superb. She brushes twice a day with an electric toothbrush, flosses religiously, and uses mouthwash with fluoride. There was no indication anything was wrong. No twinges of pain in her jaw or mouth. No loose teeth. No bleeding gums.

Her phone dings. It's an email from Marjorie, checking in on her, and Elle's heart warms. Marjorie is an exceptional manager, the kind of woman who is more of a mentor than a boss. She's encouraging and supportive while also embodying the kind of tough-as-nails, take-no-shit businesswoman Elle endeavors to become.

As Elle reads the email, her heart soars and then plummets. Marjorie tells her to take the rest of the week off, which is a relief. She has no idea what the timeline for her procedures or recovery will look like. It's the next statement that brings frustrated tears to Elle's eyes. Marjorie explains that Kyle, a colleague on Elle's team, will deliver the rest of her presentation.

Elle sits on the lip of the bathtub, the phone heavy in her hands. She knows Marjorie means for this to be comforting. She can hear her boss's soothing voice as she reads. *Don't worry about the presentation. Rest up. You're not letting anyone down.*

But…Elle has worked so hard on this presentation. She'd hoped it would be her moment to be noticed by the higher-ups. She'd imagined presenting their team's new marketing strategy with such panache that everyone would remember her name. Perhaps Marjorie would even give her a raise.

Now, Kyle gets to deliver the new strategy, and Elle will certainly be remembered, but not for her work. She'll be remembered as that employee who lost a tooth in the middle of a managerial meeting. Disappoint careens through Elle, stabbing her heart and tightening her chest.

She sets her phone down and brings her forehead to her fingertips. She massages her temples, trying to relieve her burgeoning stress and disappointment.

When she straightens, something tumbles onto her tongue. Something solid with sharp ridges.

Elle spits the object into her palm and closes her fist without looking at it. She already knows what's happened, but she doesn't want to see it. Doesn't want to acknowledge that this has happened again. She squeezes her eyes shut, her body trembling, and hot tears stream down her cheeks while the taste of blood fills her mouth.

Bone-deep exhaustion coupled with an overwhelming feeling of helplessness had inspired Elle to call her general practitioner and request a full blood panel analysis two months earlier. The day she'd called, she'd awoken at three in the morning, slick with sweat, her skin hot to the touch. Despite wearing nothing save a light, cotton slip dress, she'd been a walking, breathing fireball.

She'd peeled her sodden nightdress from her clammy skin as droplets of sweat fell to her hardwood bedroom floor. *Guess I'll be mopping again,* she'd thought as she deposited her clothes in the washing machine.

Elle had stared at the splotchy, abstract imprint of her body that had leached into her sheets until the embarrassment tunneling through her grew too great. She felt the white-hot shame of a young girl who'd wet the bed—which, she guessed, was an accurate statement.

She'd cried in the shower, because she was tired. Tired of doing laundry multiple nights a week. Tired of living in a body that was suddenly unpredictable. Tired of turning down social engagements, because she was consumed with fear over this rogue body she was trapped within.

Even when Elle described her symptoms—persistent night sweats, vaginal dryness accompanied by fine cuts on her labia, an erratic menstrual cycle despite being on birth control—her doctor had assured her that she was far too young for her discomforts to be attributed to something like perimenopause. Was she experiencing great levels of stress in her work or home life? Was she on any new medications or experimenting with recreational drugs? Had she been consuming more alcohol recently?

Elle answered these questions calmly and truthfully, and again stated that she wanted a blood panel. She didn't care if it would be covered by her insurance. She wanted answers. Her doctor had harumphed, stating that she thought Elle's request was overkill—until the results came back.

Elle's LDL cholesterol was higher than the doctor would've liked, and her thyroid activity was slightly irregular. Coupled with the symptoms she'd reported, well, did perimenopause run in her family? Had she ever received cancer treatments? Had she ever had her ovaries checked?

There had been no logical explanation. Elle's body had simply revolted and begun to change.

And so, she'd been thrust headlong into treatment discussions. Over-the-counter lubricants and vaginal estrogen tablets to alleviate down-there dryness. Estrogen skin patches to help balance her hormone levels and relieve her gamut of symptoms. Prescriptions for antidepressants, which could reduce the severity of her hot flashes and also provide emotional balance and support during this "delicate transition."

The doctor also mentioned the importance of a quality diet and calcium supplements since menopausal women often experienced osteoporosis. If she wasn't careful, Elle could experience significant bone loss.

Elle has a lot to say, but she can't bring herself to call her doctor's office. With the loss of her second tooth, her speech is severely slurred. She sounds pitiable. Or drunk. She can't decide which is worse.

Her fingers fly over her laptop keyboard, typing out a message for her doctor. Per her healthcare plan's protocol, she'll receive a response from someone on her care team within 24 hours. By then, she'll have seen her dentist, Dr. Mowry, and she'll have even more information to share.

She hits send and watches her long-winded message disappear into the ether. Now, there's nothing left to do but wait. Though perhaps...

Elle has a sudden inclination to drink a glass of milk. She knows this action is too little, too late—tantamount to taking a big dose of vitamin C *after* you detect the first symptoms of a cold—but it will give her something to do. And if it makes her feel even a little better, it will be worth it.

She freezes when she opens the fridge, suddenly confronted by the glass of milk that holds her lost teeth. One tooth is pressed against the bottom of the cup, its jagged edge kissing the glass. The image reminds Elle of a macabre boba milk tea, and the tableau is so unsettling, her hands are numb as she fumbles past containers of leftovers to find the carton of milk.

She fills a glass and chugs, ignoring the rivulets of milk that escape the lip of the cup and drip down her chin. Elle imagines the liquid calcium swimming through the cracks in her teeth, fortifying bone with every splash. Her stomach gurgles as she places the empty cup on the counter. Feelings of calm and accomplishment weave through her body.

And that's when she notices the man standing on the sidewalk in front of her house. She can make out his silhouette through the slats of her blinds, a dark spot hovering behind the white vinyl. Though Elle knows he can't see her, she takes a small step to her right, away from the window.

What is he doing? Elle wonders as she observes the man. He assumes a casual stance, hands in pockets, shoulders relaxed, sunglasses protecting his eyes from the midafternoon sun. She watches as the man sweeps her front yard with a lingering gaze and then turns and walks away.

He was lost, Elle tells herself, even as her core trembles and her pulse races. *The house numbers are hard to make out on this block. He's someone's guest. A friend. It's fine. You're fine, Elle.*

She stands in her kitchen for another ten minutes, gazing out the window, waiting for the man to reappear, but he never does.

You can't stand here all day, Elle reasons and pulls herself away from the window. She opens her fridge, does her best to ignore the cup of lost teeth in milk, and reaches for a glass bottle in the very back. She unscrews the top, tips back her head, and lets a few drops of CBD oil nestle beneath her tongue. She changes into shorts and a tank top and props herself up against a small mountain of pillows in bed.

She prays for sleep.

Elle is drowning. She flails and gasps, desperate to fill her lungs with oxygen, but something hard and immovable is blocking her throat.

She wakes to darkness, twisted up in bedsheets, her mouth full of sharpness and iron. Elle rolls to her side, spits, and sucks in fresh air. After a few breaths, she grinds her face into her pillows, trying to rid her skin of blood and saliva and knowing.

The bright taste of copper brings hot tears to her eyes. She lets her tongue rove and mentally maps the inside of her mouth. Her exploratory movements confirm her worst fears. There are far too many empty chasms within. She imagines her mouth a living cemetery, studded with tombstones of brittle bone, surrounded by withering, pink flesh.

Elle needs to get to the bathroom. She needs to see the full extent of the damage. Then, she'll drive to the emergency room. Two lost teeth are bad enough, but now Elle's situation has escalated into a scene out of a horror film.

She flings the sheets from her body and is about to stand when she hears a floorboard creak. Not a floorboard under her own feet, but one down the hall, closer to her kitchen. Elle freezes. Waits. Listens.

This is simply the house settling, right? She closes her eyes, hoping the house will groan and she can confirm her hypothesis that this noise is the stretching of its ancient bones.

But the unmistakable sound of a footfall meets Elle's ears, followed by a creak as wood strains beneath the weight of a body. Another footfall, another screech.

Someone is in the house.

Elle's heart punches against her ribs, and she gropes in the dark for the phone on her bedside table. The device lights up at her touch. She keys in the number for emergency services and she brings her shaking hand to her ear.

"9-1-1, what's your emergency?"

"There's someone in my house." This is what Elle wants to whisper into the receiver, but her checkerboard mouth refuses to form the words. Instead, breathy, wet noises spill from her bludgeoned maw.

"Can you repeat that, please?" The words are crisp and unhurried. Easily expelled. Infuriatingly so.

Two more steps sound in the hall. The intruder is nearing Elle's bedroom. And what will she do if they enter? Elle knows she should get up. She should run to her closet, lock herself inside, and try to better communicate with this emergency operator.

But her body won't cooperate, and it's no surprise. Elle's body hasn't been cooperating for months.

"What's your emergency?"

Elle's thoughts turn inward. What *is* her emergency?

She is perimenopausal, a slave to sweat and hormones and crumbling bones. She's lost an unknown quantity of teeth, and with them, she's lost opportunity, dignity, nerve, and her voice. And now, she's in danger, a caged animal, wounded and waiting and unable to move.

An urgency blooms within Elle's belly, edged with anger. The feeling is primordial and otherworldly. She opens her mouth and lets go, howling into the phone, a desperate, heartbroken wailing. A coyote cry. A scream that begs for survival, for someone to care.

Please, please, don't leave me behind.

The Last Woman

I want to feel all of you,
He says,
And his voice is an oil slick,
Intent on staining my skin
With blood and bad intentions.

I smile, knowing he's about to get much more than he
paid for,
And then I oblige,
Allowing cotton, then silk, then bone
Fall to the floor.
He tries to run, except
There's nowhere to go but
Down, down, down.

He stares into my throat as I approach,
And the pink folds invite him in,
Head, shoulders, knees, and toes.
He tastes of skinned knees,

Uncauterized wounds,
Protests muffled by hotel pillows.

My esophagus welcomes him into its slippery embrace,
And I can feel him scream as peristalsis kicks in.
Contract, relax.
Contract, relax.

My body purrs when he's finally submerged and
Gastric juices break him down,
Churning and burning till he's mine,
Nothing more than chyme.

I absorb his rage, his power, his sadness,
All the things he used to employ
To unwillingly pin others beneath him.
I convulse and contort,
Taking him in,
Swallowing his poison.

Afterward, I lay on the hotel mattress,
Trembling, coming down from the high,
Naked and smoking and soaked in sweat.

I think of the shoes I'll buy
With the crumpled-up cash on the nightstand,
Blood money turned beautiful,
And lick my lips.

When I'm finally sated and still,
I smile, imagining him
And the way he looked
When he realized I was the last woman
He'd ever fuck
With.

Murder Memory

When Justine glided into Room 304B, the relief she felt at being far, far removed from her everyday life was immediate and absolute.

After depositing her suitcase on the bed, she removed her white lace gloves and strolled leisurely along the perimeter of the room. Her fingertips traced the Gothic pattern etched on the wallpaper, delighting in its texture and warmth. She smiled at the immaculate furniture that looked as if it had been plucked from an old English estate, then bent to smell the sweet perfume of a vase of exquisite, blood-red roses.

Justine hadn't visited in over a year, but the suite was exactly as she remembered it. And if her memory continued to serve her correctly, she'd feel rejuvenated, restored, and nourished—body, mind, and soul—by the end of her stay.

Here at *Les Coeurs des Tous,* there was no internet connection. No work emails could reach her, no matter how urgent. The rotary-style phone within Justine's room would only connect her with the front desk. It would not accept outside phone calls. Neither her husband nor her children could call her—though, they thought she was on a girls' camping trip with friends, so they wouldn't try to reach her anyway.

The only interactions Justine would have over the next three days would be with the exceptional staff at *Les Coeurs*. And they were there to cater to her every whim. For a brief time, no one would require anything of Justine; however, she could require *everything* of others. The thought sent a delicious thrill down her spine.

Justine closed her eyes and breathed in the smell of the room—the earthy aroma of antique furniture, the sterile scents of bleach and cleaning solution, and there, beneath it all, an odor only identifiable to those of Justine's ilk—the subtle tang of iron. She smiled.

A loud crash sounded from the suite next door. Justine pressed her ear against the lush wallpaper and listened for a while, her heart racing, her mind reeling.

When she could take it no longer, Justine strode purposefully to the other side of the suite and dialed the front desk.

"Miss Monroe, my name is Carson. What can I do for you this afternoon?"

"Hello, Carson. I'm calling about my neighbors, the ones in 305B?"

"Yes, ma'am. Lovely couple. They checked in this morning."

"They seem to be having quite a good time. I'm assuming the staff provided them with their afternoon entertainment?"

"Yes, ma'am."

"Excuse me for being so forward, but is there any chance I could have what they're having?" Justine heard the sound of paper ruffling over the line. She held her breath, hoping for good news.

"You're in luck, Miss Monroe. We have another. Would you like us to charge the entertainment to your room?"

"Yes, please. Cost is not an issue."

"And shall you be dining afterward?"

"Yes. I believe you have my preparation preferences?"

"Of course, ma'am. We have on file that you prefer your meat cooked medium rare. Is that still your preference?"

"Yes."

"Very good. Will you be requiring any weapons this evening?"

"No, thank you. I've brought my own."

"Very good, ma'am. I have the utmost respect for well-prepared women."

Justine blushed at the compliment. This Carson fellow would receive a great tip.

The man on the phone continued. "As always, necessary supplies can be found in your closet. We appreciate you abiding by the hotel's rules and regulations to keep your room as clean as possible."

"Of course," Justine said.

"Very good. When would you like the entertainment delivered to your room?"

"Is an hour too soon?"

"Not at all. We're happy to oblige...Oh, I have a fine suggestion, ma'am."

"Yes?"

"Just this morning, we received a case of truly superb Australian Malbec. It pairs most excellently with red meat. Would you like us to bring you a bottle with your meal?"

Justine's mouth watered. "That sounds divine."

"Wonderful. I'll add it to your bill."

Justine heard the distinct *clack-clack-clack* of a typewriter, then Carson's voice warmed the line. "I'll ring you when our afternoon handler, Brandon, is on his way up. Would you like any details about your prey, Miss Monroe?"

"No, thank you. I do love a surprise."

Carson chuckled. "I knew I liked you, ma'am. Is there anything else you require at this time?"

"I think that'll do it. Thank you so much for your help. I truly appreciate it."

Justine hung up the receiver of the old-timey phone and smoothed her silk skirt. She had an hour to herself, the perfect amount of time to ready both the room and her nerves. She was exhilarated, yes, but also a little anxious. It had been a while since her last kill. What with the responsibilities of being a wife, a mother, and a corporate professional, she simply hadn't had the time to satisfy her innermost desires with any sort of regularity.

Justine hoped she still remembered how to do this. Like muscle memory, but instead...*murder* memory. She let out a carefree, high-pitched giggle at her pun.

Justine unzipped her suitcase and extracted her collection of knives. As Carson had promised, plastic sheeting, rolls of duct tape, and gloves lined the walk-in closet, beautifully organized and of the highest quality, because, of course, that was the way at *Les Coeurs*.

Whistling a jaunty tune, Justine set to work preparing 304B, her body humming in anticipation.

The Gift

As I watched the blinking lights from a holiday display dance across my husband's face, I imagined bashing his skull in with the Pyrex dish of lasagna I held.

Wes licked his lips and began whistling "Oh, Little Town of Bethlehem," the high notes cutting through the dark. His gray eyes remained fixed on our destination, Mrs. Potter's house at the end of the street, where her annual Christmas party was in full swing.

After weeks of tamping down suspicions and navigating quiet, covert panic attacks, I'd finally broached the topic. And now, he was ignoring my question. Anger bubbled within me. He was either pretending not to have heard me, or he was stalling.

And though his evasion spoke volumes, I needed to hear the truth from his lips. I had to get an answer out of him before we got to the party, where inevitably, we would be swallowed up by holiday music and spiked eggnog and the godawful white elephant gift exchange everyone in the neighborhood pretended to love because it brought Mrs. Potter so much joy. All that holiday cheer would eat me alive.

"Wes." I stopped in the middle of the street.

He took another two steps before expelling a huge sigh and turning, the soles of his shoes scratching against asphalt. "How am I supposed to know, Beth?" Wes's voice was low and razor sharp. He shrugged his shoulders and pinned me with his eyes.

I instinctively wilted beneath his gaze, my shoulders rounding forward, but then I caught myself. *Fuck, no. I'm not going to cave.* I stood tall and pressed my chest forward. I allowed venom to taint my voice. "I thought perhaps she'd mentioned it to you."

"And why would she do that?"

Because you two apparently talk about everything, I wanted to say. *I've watched you. Through the bay window in the kitchen, early in the morning when you think I'm still asleep. She pretends to trim her rosebushes. You drink your first cup of coffee of the day. You laugh and laugh.*

A shock of pain flashed through my jaw. I was clenching my teeth. I let out a gust of breath, which fogged in the cold night air. I shook my head and stared down at my cranberry-colored boots. Why had I hoped for honesty? I should've known he'd deny, deny, deny.

"Fine. You want to know what Carrie made for the party?" Wes asked. "Chocolate chip cookies."

My head snapped up and that desire to strike him again snaked through my arms, hot and ready. Wes stood there in the middle of the road, his chest puffed, his hands casually slung in the pockets of his woolen coat. His eyes were narrowed at me, his expression daring me to say something.

He cocked his head to the side and shifted his gaze to the stars. "Oh wait, or was it prosciutto-wrapped melon she's bringing?"

Sarcasm dripped like syrup from his lips. "Buckeyes? Maybe it was Mexican wedding cookies."

I launched forward and shoved the Pyrex against his chest. He stumbled back a couple steps, and his hands flew from his pockets to receive the dish. "You're an asshole," I said.

I stomped toward Mrs. Potter's beautifully lit home, the tears in my eyes rendering the decorations a kaleidoscope of red, green, and white.

The first five minutes in Mrs. Potter's house felt like a bad dream. The whole place smelled of peppermint, a scent I generally loved but which had recently begun to turn my stomach. Everyone wore overstretched smiles that made it appear as if their faces were about to split right down the middle. And the constant cacophony of jovial conversation, plastic forks scratching against plastic plates, and Bing Crosby singing "White Christmas" made me twitchy.

Wes and I had split up, of course. He was off somewhere—with Carrie, no doubt, doing God knows what—while I clutched a cup of hot apple cider and exchanged pleasantries with Mrs. Potter. I smiled and nodded as she told me about how morning glories had overtaken her backyard and she really needed to hire someone to remove them.

Hire someone to remove them. Yes, that seemed very logical. I imagined a landscaper cutting back Mrs. Potter's morning glories with a gigantic set of shears and then crossing the street to snip Wes right out of my life.

If only it were that simple.

A soft warble brought me back to my conversation with Mrs. Potter. "Hmm?"

"Are you feeling alright, dear? You look flushed."

And she was right. During the course of our chat, a layer of sweat had wound its way across my arms and chest, trying to cool the hot skin that lay under my festive cardigan. I was feeling a bit insubstantial, like butter that had softened on the counter for too long.

"I am a little warm," I said.

Mrs. Potter's eyes darted downward, and when I realized what she was looking at, I removed my hand my belly and shoved it in my jeans pocket.

Damn. Damn, damn, damn.

Mrs. Potter's eyes met mine, and I was overwhelmed by the warmth and understanding there. "If you need a break, you can use the bathroom in the back of the house, through my bedroom. It's down the hall, last door on the right. No one will bother you there."

I sniffed to keep my emotions in check. Mrs. Potter eased the cup of cider from my hand. The pressure of her palm on my lower back was comforting as she ushered me away from the Christmas cheer.

I'd been told time and time again that I couldn't get pregnant. And yet, five separate at-home tests had told me otherwise earlier in the week. I'd crumpled to the bathroom floor and sobbed, half out of disbelief and half out of pure joy.

I'd taken the tests on a lark. My period was only a few days late, but I thought perhaps this time would be different.

I'd done the calculations in my head, and I figured I was about a month and a half along. Blessedly, my symptoms were mild—a little nausea here and there, a touch of dizziness, small discomforts that were easy to attribute to cold and flu season.

I needed to tell Wes. I had a doctor's appointment the following week, and I knew he'd be excited about the pregnancy. He craved fatherhood and wanted to gather a child up in his arms as much as I did—but I had to clear up my suspicions about him and his early morning chats with Carrie first.

If Wes was cheating, I didn't want a baby to be the glue that put us back together. I knew that bond would be fickle. It would erode over time.

No, this child *would not* be a Band-Aid for our relationship. Wes needed to want both of us.

I stared at my reflection in the glass, at my deep brown eyes, my coiffed hair, my cheery Christmas cardigan. I was beautiful and more than worthy, dammit. If Wes couldn't see that, or if he'd been tempted by something new, well, I could do without him in my life.

Fresh resolve bloomed within me, and I made a plan. We'd hash this out tonight, after the party. I'd be direct. Cool. Calm. And I knew what I would do if he'd been unfaithful.

After a few more deep breaths, I exited Mrs. Potter's bathroom and returned to the party. The fete was easier to enjoy this time around. I ate sugar cookies dusted in red and green sugar. I chatted with the Browns, whose son was about to go off to college. Mariah Carey sang about all she wanted for Christmas.

When Mrs. Potter turned down the music and announced it was time for the white elephant gift exchange, I scanned the room. Wes still wasn't there, and anxiety skittered through my veins. I told Mrs. Potter I'd round up any guests who were in the backyard, tell them it was time.

Cold air bit my skin when I stepped onto the patio. There were a few partygoers outside, bundled up, seated at a table, smoking and drinking. "Time for the white elephant gift exchange," I said, gesturing behind me. The smokers stubbed out their cigarettes, gathered their drinks, and stepped inside.

Neither Wes nor Carrie had been among them, but something in my gut told me they weren't far, though the yard was quiet and still.

I let my boots scape against the concrete as I moved back toward the house. I opened Mrs. Potter's sliding glass door and then shut it so that it sounded as if I'd gone back inside. And then I listened.

Was that a sigh I heard off in the corner of the yard? A whisper? The creak of wood?

As quietly as I could, I tiptoed off the patio and onto the grass. There, I paused and listened, hoping my movements hadn't given me away.

A bright giggle sliced through the night air, and my knees buckled. I bent over, my hands braced on my thighs, my lungs suddenly desperate for oxygen. The shaking started in my chest and spread down my arms, through my pelvis, and into my extremities. That giggle, with its high pitch and sing-song quality, was Carrie's.

I knew in my bones I was about to catch Wes in the act. Did I want this? Did I have the strength? And what would I do when I caught them together?

Too bad I don't have that lasagna dish.

Tears stung my eyes, but I squeezed them away. Now was not the time. Not for dark humor *or* falling apart.

A shuffling sound drew my gaze to the rusted shed in the corner of the yard. It was a perfect metal square, about seven feet tall and seven feet wide. Just tall enough to hide a six-foot-two man.

I crept across the grass and flattened myself against the front of the shed. I sidestepped to the corner and there it was, the sounds of clothing swishing, lips meeting, low moaning.

They'd hidden in the crevice formed by the side of the shed and Mrs. Potter's wooden fence. Carrie was pressed against corrugated metal, her fingers threaded through Wes's hair. He kissed her with a desire and urgency I didn't know he was capable of feeling. His hands pulled her hips into him, causing her back to arch.

My whole body went cold. I watched as my husband desperately grabbed and caressed another woman. Something inside me cracked in two.

Wes broke away from Carrie's lips and began kissing her neck, nipping her skin with his teeth.

"That feels so good, Wes," Carrie said. "Keep doing that."

Wes tugged at the neckline of Carrie's sweater and attacked her clavicle with his lips. Carried tossed her head back, presenting her skin to him, her eyes closed.

Okay, you've seen enough. Leave. Run back inside. Get the hell out of here.

But I was frozen to the spot like a gargoyle, watching my husband ravage our neighbor.

Carrie licked her lips as Wes continued his ministrations. And then she licked her lips again and again and again. By the fourth lick, I could've sworn her tongue had lengthened substantially, enough so that it reached past her lips and tickled the cleft in her chin.

I closed my eyes and shook my head. *It's a Christmas light playing across her face. Or your imagination creating ridiculous visions. You're in shock. Shock, shock, shock.*

When I opened my eyes and took in the scene anew, I sank to my knees, gripping the edge of the shed. Carrie's tongue darted in and out of her mouth in quick succession. Each time it escaped her lips, the muscle stretched further and further into the night, its tip diverging into two parts, forking like a snake's. Her hands clutched the back of Wes's head, pressing his face against her skin. Her eyes now glowed in the dark, a piercing yellow color.

I knew I should run. Seek help. At the very least, intervene before something terrible happened.

Because something terrible was definitely about to happen. I could feel it in my marrow.

But there was also a primal instinct within me that said, *Stay. Watch.* It was so powerful, this suggestion to linger, that

I remained rooted there in the dark, observing the scene as an emotional cocktail of horror, fascination, and grief coursed through me.

Carrie's tongue continued to flick skyward, as if she was attempting to catch stars with every pass. Each time, her tongue stretched and extended, shooting higher and higher into the night sky, until I could no longer see its forked anatomy in the dim.

"God, I want you," Wes gasped against her flesh.

"I want you, too," Carried whispered—and then she struck. She yanked Wes's face from her chest, and her enormous tongue wound itself around his neck until all I could see was the color pink. Wes wheezed as the massive rope cut off his air supply. His hands flew to his neck, and he scrabbled against Carrie's hold. His eyes bulged, and I was afraid they might pop out of their sockets. The smell of urine spiked the air, and a dark spot bloomed on Wes's jeans.

I clamped a hand to my mouth and bit back bile.

As Wes struggled and kicked, trying to escape Carrie's grasp, she stood strong and steady, her yellow eyes cold and unblinking. It didn't take long, less than a minute. Wes's thrashing grew weaker and weaker until he hung limp from Carrie's tongue, twitching. When he'd stilled, the pink scarf unwound from his neck and retracted into Carrie's mouth.

She stripped him, tossing his shoes, jeans, Christmas sweater, and underwear into a heap nearby. She lowered herself to the concrete, sitting on her knees, and bowed forward so her chin rested on the ground near Wes's head. Carrie opened her mouth wide, and I watched in horror as her jaw unhinged, allowing her maw to stretch wide. Too wide. Carrie's forked tongue whipped out, looped around Wes's neck, and began pulling him into her awaiting mouth.

It wasn't until Carrie had hauled half of Wes's corpse down her throat that I was able to tear my gaze from the scene. My ass hit the concrete and I leaned hard against the shed.

What the fuck had I just witnessed? I'd watched my husband's lover strangle and then *eat* him, right? And what exactly was Carrie? Clearly, she wasn't human. Or at least, not entirely. Was she part snake? A snake-woman?

The sound of footsteps kicked my thoughts to the wayside. Carrie had finished feeding, and now she was approaching.

"Beth?" Carrie's voice was calm and sweet, a stark contrast to what I'd just witnessed. She peered down at me. Her eyes had returned to their regular blue color, and she looked incredible, not a hair out of place. No indication that she was...what, a monster?

I dug my boots into the ground and pressed my back against the shed, wishing I could melt into the metal and escape. Because I needed to get away. I knew what Carrie was capable of, and I didn't want to be her next meal.

The snake-woman held Wes's clothes, neatly folded, between her palms. She crouched, and I closed my eyes, turned my head away, and clutched my stomach. I waited. But nothing happened.

When I reopened my eyes, Carrie was there, crouching, holding out Wes's clothes to me. I looked at the garments, and repulsion shuddered through me. I shook my head. I didn't want them.

Carrie licked her lips with a very human tongue. "I'm really sorry you saw that. I guess you know now."

Was she referring to her and Wes's affair? Or her ability to eat humans whole? I guess I knew about both, so I nodded.

Carrie cocked her head to the side and frowned. "You're pregnant."

My eyes widened, and I pulled my knees to my chest protectively. "How did you...?"

Carrie smiled. "I can smell it."

I gulped down cold air. Were women who were expecting a child more delicious than others?

"It's okay, Beth. I'd never hurt you."

I searched her eyes for malice or deception, but found only truth and compassion. Which was weird, since she was a murderer and all.

"I only feed on those who hurt others. People with deceit in their hearts. I only eat darkness. Do you understand?"

I nodded dumbly. What else could I do?

She tucked Wes's clothes under one armpit and held out her other hand to me. "Can I help you up?"

I stared at her hand, expecting to see scales, but only creamy skin caught the sparse light.

"I won't hurt you."

I grasped her hand, and she hoisted me up far too easily, an act that hinted at her preternatural strength.

I stood there, staring into Carrie's face. Her features melted away as I recalled what had happened only moments ago. Wes's face, bloated and pale, his air being squeezed from his lungs with Carrie's giant tongue. I saw his naked body disappearing inch by inch down our neighbor's throat, and I shuddered.

He was gone. Wes was gone forever.

And then I started to cry, not because I was disgusted or scared, but because relief poured through me.

The snake-woman wrapped me in her arms and held me.

Carrie and I were extremely late to the white elephant gift exchange, but Mrs. Potter waved us over and demanded we participate. I thought I'd be a wreck, unable to function, but the collective cheer in Mrs. Potter's house combined with the fact that I had cried everything out on Carrie's shoulder gave me a temporary boost of energy and spirit.

I wound up with a set of star-shaped cookie cutters and a pack of hot chocolate. Carrie received a holiday gift pack of fancy barbecue spices, which I found particularly hilarious.

As soon as the gift exchange wrapped up, I knew it was time to go home. I had a lot to process. A lot to plan.

"Where's that husband of yours?" Mrs. Potter asked as I shrugged on my coat. She handed me my lasagna dish, freshly washed.

"I told him the news, and he bolted."

Mrs. Potter frowned, her lips puckered, and I swore I could see smoke streaming out of her ears like one of those characters in old-timey cartoons.

I placed a hand on her shoulder. "It's okay. It's better this way, honestly." It was the truth, but it was still difficult to say aloud. Emotion swelled within me, and I gritted my teeth to keep it from pouring forth. I swiped fresh tears from my eyes and collected Mrs. Potter's hand in my own. "But I may need some help."

Mrs. Potter's face brightened. She filled her lungs with air and smiled. "Anything you need." She squeezed my hands, and warmth filled me. "In fact— " She held up a finger and puttered away into the kitchen.

As I waited, Carrie approached and collected her coat. Her movements were so smooth and fluid. Like a dance. How had I never noticed?

At Mrs. Potter's door, she turned. "You're going to be okay, Beth. I can tell."

I gave her a nod, and she slipped into the night. Somehow, I knew I would never see her again.

Mrs. Potter returned with a plate heaped with food from the party—a square of my own lasagna, lemon bars, a slice of cheesecake, meatballs, gingerbread cookies, and caprese salad. She winked as she passed me the dish.

At home, I put a slice of cheesecake on a plate and heated milk for hot chocolate. With only the glow of the Christmas tree to keep me company, I sat on the couch, chewing and sipping in silence. The absence of Wes hung heavy, a thick fog of what had come to pass and what could have been. But I knew the weight of his memory would lessen over time, just as the scent of pine from our fresh Christmas tree would dissipate after the holiday season.

The lights on the tree twinkled and danced, and I turned my thoughts to the new life growing inside me—small, strong, safe.

Happiness washed over me, fresh as snow, and I knew that Carrie was right.

I was going to be okay.

Content Warnings

- The Price of Motherhood – infertility issues, body horror/gore

- Heavy Is the Head – none

- Something Black – sexual harassment (minor)

- Pursuit - stalking

- The Girl Who Lost Herself – fatphobia (parent toward a child), cultural appropriation, cultural fetishization

- Heartless – body horror/gore

- Extraction – blemish/zit-related body horror/gore, beauty standards

- My Love, In Pieces – domestic violence

- This Woman's Work – body horror, domestic violence

- Seeing Double – rape culture

- Forever Longing – none

- The Wailing – body horror, home invasion

- The Last Woman – violence against sex workers (minor, implied)

- Murder Memory – none

- The Gift – infertility issues

Publication History

"The Price of Motherhood" originally appeared in *ProleSCAR Yet: Tales of Horror and Class Warfare,* Rad Flesh Press, May 2021.

"Heavy Is the Head" is original to this collection.

"Something Black" originally appeared in *Zen of the Dead,* Popcorn Press, November 2015.

"Pursuit" is original to this collection.

"The Girl Who Lost Herself" is original to this collection.

"Heartless" is original to this collection.

"Extraction" is original to this collection.

"My Love, In Pieces" originally appeared in *Quoth the Raven: A Contemporary Reimagining of the Words of Edgar Allan Poe*, Camden Park Press, October 2018. This story was also adapted to audio by the NoSleep Podcast, Season 13, Episode 21.

"This Woman's Work" originally appeared on the *Spreading the Writer's Word* blog, Nina D'Arcangelo.

"Seeing Double" is original to this collection.

"Forever Longing" originally appeared in *Handmade Horror Stories: An Anthology of Art and Craft Themed Short Horror Fiction*, Frost Zone Press, September 2021.

"The Wailing" is original to this collection.

"The Last Woman" originally appeared in *Under Her Skin: A Women in Horror Poetry Collection, Volume 1*, Black Spot Books, April 2022.

"Murder Memory" originally appeared on the *Spreading the Writer's Word* blog, Nina D'Arcangelo.

"The Gift" originally appeared on the Fright Girl Summer website. It was also adapted to audio on the Voices From the Mausoleum YouTube channel, Spooky Sunday Stories, December 2022.

Acknowledgments

This collection has been a long time coming, and I truly couldn't have done it without the support of so many.

Thank you Sonora for your friendship, encouragement, and belief in my work. Our monthly chats and erotic thriller buddy-watches are always a highlight for me. You bring so much laughter and light into my life. And hey, I have a podcast now, so let Will know we'll have the opportunity to record some of our delightfully unhinged and hilarious commentary on life, baking, and celebrity gossip.

Thank you to the creative brain trust I've been lucky enough to stumble into these past few months. Alexis, Eric, Alex, Adrian, Shelley, Sofia, Christi, Angela, Jen, Ava, and Zach, y'all are gems. Thank you for the life chats, micro fiction writing sprints, witchcraft, encouragement, beta reads, and all-around coolness. I'm happy to have each of you in my life and in my corner.

Thank you to Zen for being the goodest boy and my early morning writing buddy. I appreciate that you recognize the importance of a cozy blanket and snacks for the creative process. Also, naps.

Thank you to my parents for always supporting my creative endeavors no matter how strange or dark or weird they may be. I finally did it; I wrote a book!

And finally, thank you to Bryan, my rock in the storm, my urban adventure partner, my favorite barista, my love. You are my safe place. You give me room to create, and you celebrate every publication, every win, with me, no matter how big or small. I think this one calls for cheesecake and champagne, yeah?

About Author

Tiffany Michelle Brown is a California-based writer who once had a conversation with a ghost over a pumpkin beer. Her fiction and poetry has been featured in publications by Black Spot Books, Dread Stone Press, Death Knell Press, Cemetery Gates Media, Cursed Morsels Press, and the NoSleep Podcast, among others. She is the co-host of the Horror in the Margins podcast, which seeks to promote indie horror media and celebrate diverse creators within the horror community. Tiffany lives near the beach with her husband Bryan, their pup Zen, and their combined collections of books, board games, and general geekery.

www.ingramcontent.com/pod-product-compliance
Lightning Source LLC
Chambersburg PA
CBHW022006170726
47994CB00023B/2283